GETTING AUSTIN

a rom-com novella

LENORE NICASTRO

STORIED EXISTENCE
PUBLISHING

Copyright © 2023 by Lenore Nicastro

All rights reserved.

ISBN: 979-8-8648-2350-7

All of the characters and certain places in this story are products of the author's imagination. Any similarity to actual places or to actual persons, living or deceased, is purely coincidental.

Cover designed with Canva.

For all my fellow MS warriors

Prologue

My eyes pop open and I see that it's light outside. I'm lying there next to him, both of us clad only in our underwear.

My left leg has a muscle spasm as I drape it over his. He doesn't stir. He stays beautifully asleep. His hair is a perfect mess that I gently touch with my right index finger before I move it down to his rough, pre-shaven chin. Then my fingertips gather to feel the contrasting creamy smoothness of his bare chest. I stop before my hand goes too far and travels to his great abs and the waistband of his boxer briefs.

I wish he'd wake up and drown me underneath him as he covers me with nuzzles. That's where it all goes away. Where I don't think about MS and the shitty things it's done to my body and my life.

But then it happens. My leg gets hit with a tremor, and then the bed starts shaking like we're in an earthquake, his whole body bursts apart like shattering glass, and I'm left lying next to the pieces. Until a giant broom swoops from above and sweeps them off the bed.

Then I wake up.

~1~

You could tell that morning how close it was to summer without looking at a calendar. It was in the air, even indoors. I wasn't quite ready for it. I kicked off my light blanket, feeling a thin layer of perspiration on my skin.

I had just woken up out of a recurring dream I'd been having for the last three or four months. It took me a few seconds to get my bearings and realize that it was morning, and that I had in fact just had the dream again. I sat up in bed and thought about what it might mean.

I figured it had something to do with the fact that I was without a boyfriend, a soul mate, a partner – whatever term you prefer to use – to be there for me, to provide emotional support when I need it, to be a shoulder to lean on or cry on. To listen when I need to talk about it, and put his arms around me to reassure me that everything will be okay.

I had no man in my life.

Unless you count Pokey, my handsome, soft, green-eyed orange and white cloud of a cat. His full name is Slowpoke (or Mr. Slowpoke, or Sir Slowpoke.) He's called that because he moves around slowly most of the time. He's not old (he's only five) and he's not overweight. I've had him since he was a kitten and he's been like this since then. He just takes his time, walking along and looking around like a little old man puttering in his garden.

I think he does it because he doesn't want to miss anything. He'll sit on the windowsill, and when he wants to come down, he steps toward the edge, then he goes back and throws another glance out the window. He does this four or five times before he finally jumps down.

I suppose I shouldn't criticize Pokey, though. I'm a slowpoke too, thanks to having multiple sclerosis. It's a crazy, unpredictable monster that lives inside me.

I have relapsing-remitting MS, which means I have occasional flare-ups where my symptoms, like the muscle spasm in my dream, get worse, or I may get a new one, like the balance issue I occasionally have now. The symptoms may lighten up after a flare, but I'm never asymptomatic.

I dragged myself out of bed after thinking about the recurring dream, and I took a shower. The warm water felt good as it soaked my skin, but heat means fatigue now, so I am exhausted after every shower.

Now that summer was closing in, the outdoor heat would be impacting me too. I just couldn't wait, sarcastically speaking.

I'm like a vampire now. Keep me out of the sun, or I'll burst into flames. All kidding aside, I can't stay out in the heat too long or I start to wilt. The fatigue makes my limbs get heavy, and I feel like I'm walking through sand.

I got out of the shower and went to sit on my bed and rest for a few minutes, wrapped in a towel. Then I got dressed and threw my damp long blonde hair into a ponytail.

At my bedroom door I picked up the cane I'd just recently begun using. It's turquoise, like my birthstone. I bought it to replace the white one I got from the physical therapy clinic.

I left my first floor apartment in a renovated older building with a flat entrance and walked to the corner coffee shop that opened last year. I'm a regular there now.

"Morning, Brad," I said to the handsome, thirty-year-old dark-haired barista behind the counter.

"Tess! Good morning, gorgeous," he replied. "The usual?"

"Yes, please." I smiled at his calling me gorgeous. His fiancée Sara has exclusive rights, but he is fun to look at - all muscular and just as steamy as the beverages he serves.

"You sure you don't want iced? It's hot out," he said.

"But it's nice and cool in here," I sighed happily.

"Okay, you got it."

Brad's known about me having MS for a while. Shortly after I first started coming into the coffee shop, he'd noticed my slower gait and asked if I was hurt.

I told him I have MS, and he'd said, "Oh, I'm sorry." Then he'd said something I often read about MS folks having people say right after they tell them they have MS - "You look good though."

I remember I had smiled and thanked him, and in a friendly way I'd said, "You look good too."

He'd kind of blushed and chuckled, and we're coffee shop friends now. He introduced me to Sara when she was there smooching him at the counter one day soon after that. She's a petite brunette who works in the corporate world and doesn't look like she'd be his type, but they actually seem to complement each other pretty well.

Brad rang up my order, and I put a couple of folded dollar bills into the tip jar. I went to sit at my "usual" table by the window, and after a minute or so, Brad came over with my latte and chocolate almond biscotti.

"Enjoy," he said, patting my shoulder.

I said, "Thanks," and I watched him go back to the counter. He does have a great butt.

As I sipped my latte, my thoughts went back to my dream. I presumed it was trying to tell me something. But what?

There was a man whose face I couldn't fully see. A mystery man. Was he someone I was with once, or maybe someone I just had a mad crush on? We were in bed together, so it had to be one of those.

I've had four guys in my life that you could call boyfriends. The second one cheated on me, and the first and third relationships just fizzled after a while. There was something missing, but I couldn't figure out what.

In any event, the three of them made no effort to try and stay with me, seeming to think I should have appreciated them more because they were apparently God's gifts to women. Yeah, being great in bed wasn't enough though.

Then there was Mark. He's six years older than I, and he wasn't quite so cocky. We were together the longest, but I broke up with him soon after I was diagnosed because the whole MS thing was obviously freaking him out. He wouldn't stop asking me questions; he was like the panicking guy in a disaster movie. I was already having a hard enough time dealing with the diagnosis, so I set him free to find someone else.

The recurring dream was definitely a stark reminder of my failed relationships and a shot at my still being single at thirty-seven.

After my diagnosis, I dated a few other guys, but I didn't want to get involved in another relationship. I gave up even on going on a date, not wanting to have to talk about the MS. The last two years had been a dry spell. The dream guy was the closest I'd gotten to a man in a long time.

But the way his body burst into pieces before he could wake up didn't make sense to me. Why didn't he just vanish?

Maybe he represented the cheater? But I hadn't thought of him in years. The other "God's gifts" had each come back into my life at separate times over the last few years, and we'd ended up sleeping together. MS or not, I wasn't interested in rekindling those

flames. They were both married now, and I was happy for them.
　He couldn't be one of them.
　Just who was this guy in my dream?

~2~

A few days before Memorial Day weekend I met Austin Reynolds. He works at the grocery store at the corner of my mom's street, which is where she met him, and his grandparents live on the same street.

My first impression of him – in a word - hot. Wavy light brown hair, hazel eyes, six feet tall, great physique. The first time I saw him it was an unseasonably humid day. He was shirtless, pushing the lawnmower in Mom's back yard, his t-shirt hanging from a pocket of his cargo shorts. We waved to each other, and leaning on my cane, I went into the house to talk to Mom.

The house I grew up in is a pretty standard four bedroom, two and a half bath colonial – white with black shutters. It's in a middle class suburban neighborhood where the houses are a little further apart, with big back yards, but not too far back from the street.

I knew we'd be listening to that lawnmower for a while.

Mom got some strawberries from the fridge, and we sat at the kitchen table. As I gazed out the window at the stunning man walking back and forth mowing the grass, Mom asked if the heat was bothering me.

"What?" I responded, startled. Then I realized she was asking about the weather, and I said, "Oh. No, it's not too bad."

Mom's a retired nurse, so she keeps close tabs on how I'm doing. She also tells everyone that I have MS, and when someone tells her they have a relative who has it, she tells me like I'm starting a club.

I was diagnosed at age thirty, after my legs went completely numb. Mom was still working then, but Dad was the first person I told about it.

When the loss of feeling that had begun in my feet a couple of weeks earlier was up to my thighs, I had finally called to talk to Mom. Dad answered the phone that morning. Mom had already left for work, so I tearfully told him what was going on.

He had used his business phone in his home office to call Mom at work, and he set up a conference call so the three of us could talk. Mom made me an appointment with a doctor in the hospital system that day, and she came with me when I went to see him.

Dad was the one who took me to the appointments when I had the diagnostic tests done though, since Mom couldn't get the time off. Mark was also busy working, so he couldn't go with me, but he was "really worried."

So it was just me and my self-employed father.

Dad stayed with me at my apartment after the MRI because I was upset that the doctor said it showed brain lesions. He didn't leave until Mark finally showed up.

The next day, Dad was there when I had the spinal tap, which I know he winced at, being on the squeamish side.

I was with Mark when I got the official diagnosis phone call, and it was after I cried on his shoulder that he went into full panic mode.

We broke up a couple of months later.

The numbness went away after a few months, but the fatigue and occasional muscle spasms are why I finally had to leave my bank teller job and go on disability just before my thirty-seventh birthday in December.

In January, Dad had a massive heart attack and died while just walking down the stairs one morning.

Mom had been in the kitchen making breakfast when she heard him fall. She'd tried to revive him while the ambulance was on the way. Her efforts and the efforts of the paramedics couldn't bring him back.

I'll never forget the phone call from Mom that morning telling me that he was gone. It was like the earth dropped from beneath me. The emotional impact his death had on me definitely exacerbated my MS, something I know he never would have wanted.

Dad was my rock in so many ways, not just when I was diagnosed, but through all the moments in my life where I needed him.

He was an accountant, and he'd been thrilled that I had wanted to study business, but he was totally supportive and understanding when I quit college because I couldn't handle the stress.

He'd listened to me, never judged me, and was never disappointed in me for any of my screw-ups, including my relationship debacles.

Dad has always been the purest example of love in my life. He had a lot of stress with his work, but he never let it affect me, my mom, or my younger sister Emily. We were the light in his life, and he was the light in ours.

Sometimes I can still feel his presence at the house. All I have to do is look out at the maple tree in the back yard, where he'd hung the bird feeder when I was little, and I think of him.

In May, Mom met Austin at the grocery store, and when he was helping her load her groceries in her car one day, he mentioned he helps his grandparents around their house sometimes. So of course my opportunistic mom offered him a side gig helping her out too.

He cuts the grass, takes out the trash, and he even unclogged the shower drain – something Dad always hated doing.

Mom introduced us that first day, which is when I saw the aforementioned hazel eyes.

We walked outside and approached Austin as he was pushing the mower back to the garage. I snuck a peek at his lean, muscular legs, my eyes moving quickly down to the sneakers he had on without socks.

We shook hands. His were surprisingly soft. I couldn't help but notice the little drops of sweat on his smooth chest, shining in the sun like pieces of glitter.

I breathed in, and in a weird primal way, his sweet natural fragrance filled my nostrils.

Then as I took a step back, I dropped my cane.

He picked it up and handed it to me.

"How long have you had MS?" Mom had told him, of course.

"Seven years," I said. "I only just started using the cane a couple months ago, but I guess it looks more like a couple minutes ago."

He actually laughed at my pathetic joke.

He threw his t-shirt back on, and I took a sly glance at one of his biceps pushing against a sleeve.

He put the lawnmower away, then he came back out of the garage and said goodbye to Mom, who told him to say hello to his grandparents.

I stood there, eagerly awaiting my goodbye.

He looked at me and said with a smile, "I'm glad we finally got to meet, Tess. Have a good day."

I responded, "You too."

As I watched him walk off down the driveway I was thinking, *Damn! Why didn't I say it was nice to finally meet him? And he has a great butt, too.*

After he left, Mom told me all about him – "He's thirty-two. He's a law student. He drives a Prius."

She sounded like she was writing his dating profile.

A couple of days later when we were talking on the phone, she told me that Austin had broken up with his girlfriend recently.

"What, are you two like BFFs now?" I teased.

~3~

Boom! Floor, meet Tess. On the first day of June, I fell in the morning when I stood up too fast and lost my balance after stooping to put Pokey's food bowl down for him. It wasn't the first time I'd lost my balance, but it was the first time I had fallen.

"Damn it!" I cried, prompting Pokey to amble over, his sweet face registering a look that asked, "Are you okay?"

"I'm okay, Poke. Go eat your breakfast," I said, scratching his ear. Then I slowly got up off the floor.

I saw my neurologist about a week later. I swear, Dr. Patrick Tanner is the hottest doctor ever. At least the hottest one I've ever seen. He's definitely hotter than my first neurologist, the one who diagnosed me, Dr. Rybicki. His retirement three years ago gifted me with the gorgeous Dr. Tanner.

Too bad he's married. As he sat down across from me, I was deep in my mind, imagining a night with him. He was all bare-chested, standing by the bed in our candlelit love nest, where I was waiting.

Before I could finish mentally undressing him, Dr. Tanner spoke, jolting me back to reality.

"It's nice how you smile here. Most people don't," he commented, which only made me smile more.

He did his little exam, during which I enjoyed feeling his hands on mine, and feeling them on my bare legs. An advantage of a summer appointment. He asked about my balance, and I told him about my fall.

"Uh-oh. Did you hurt yourself?" he asked like I was a little girl. It's kind of cute when he talks like that.

"No," I practically giggled.

He typed up some notes on his computer, then looking at the screen he said, "So, your first infusion is coming up."

I was going to be starting a new monthly MS medication soon. I'd been on a different medication once where I had to get weekly injections, but I'd quit that one after two months. I'm a quitter.

"Will you be doing the infusions for me?" I asked.

"No," he laughed. "The nurses at the infusion center will do them. But you knew that." He said that with his sexy sweetness.

I frowned. Can't blame a girl for trying.

That night we had a big storm that knocked the power out for a couple of hours. I lay in bed that whole time cursing the heat and not being able to have my little bedside fan on.

I have air conditioners in my apartment, but I don't use them at night to save on power.

I was fantasizing about Dr. Tanner again, which I was hoping would lead to him showing up in my dreams, but instead I had the recurring dream. Maybe the mystery guy with the hot body was Dr. Tanner?

I went over to Mom's the following afternoon. It was a Friday. Pulling into the driveway, I saw Austin on top of the garage. He was lifting one end of a long branch that I guessed the storm must have knocked down from the green apple tree behind it.

Mom came out of the house, and we walked toward the garage. As Austin was lowering the branch to the ground, I noticed the maple tree next to the garage was the one it had come from, not the green apple tree.

"Oh, no! Not the maple!" I cried.

Austin smiled as he came down the ladder from the garage roof. "Your favorite?"

I smiled back. "Yeah."

I've always loved the trees in the back yard. The maple has the best spot, being closest to the house, while the green apple and a black walnut are hidden behind the garage. We have a couple of scrappy oaks too, that stand like sentinels in front of a wall of shrubs at the very back of the yard.

Austin told Mom the garage roof looked to be intact as I walked over to the maple. Then he came over to it.

I said, "At least the branch with the bird feeder on it didn't come down."

"The feeder's empty though," Austin observed.

I asked Mom if she had any bird seed.

"No, I'm all out," she said.

"I can bring you some from the store tomorrow," Austin offered.

"That's okay, I'll just pick some up next time I come in," Mom told him.

She went over to her peonies then, and I said to Austin, "My dad was the one who always kept the feeder full."

While Mom's thing is her pond with the koi, Dad always fed the birds all year.

"Oh, he liked birds, huh?" I heard Austin say.

"Yeah."

"Yeah, I do too," he said. Then he added, "I'm sorry you lost your dad."

"Thank you," I said.

I think he noticed I was trying not to cry. He looked around, then he sighed, "I should probably get going." He called over to Mom, "Rose, I'll come back to cut this branch up and put it in the trash on Tuesday, okay?"

"Okay, sweetie," she called back.

"There's another branch that's hanging down a little, dropping apples on the roof up there," he added, pointing back to the garage.

Mom asked, "Oh, do you think you can work on that next week too?"

"Sure," he answered, tossing me a grin.

"You walked right into that one," I joked.

"Yeah," he admitted, still grinning.

We waved to each other, and I walked back to the house.

The air conditioning felt good as I came in. In the alcove off the kitchen, where my dad's home office is, I looked at the pictures on his desk.

There were Mom and Dad outside standing in front of the maple, Dad's arms around Mom as he gazed at her lovingly. Then there were all four of us – Mom, Dad, me, and Emily, sitting in the grass by Mom's flowerbed when I was twelve and Emily was five – all of us smiling for the camera.

There were more pictures sitting on top of the long credenza in front of the window. I smiled down at the ones of me and Dad before Emily came along. There I was riding on his shoulders at the zoo, sitting next to him at his desk with a big cheesy grin on my face, and in another, hanging upside down from a branch on the maple while Dad filled the feeder.

My favorite picture was the biggest one – me and Dad at a baseball game when I was seven. Mom had taken it. It was one of the few times she came to a game with us. She was pregnant with Emily then.

She had captured a perfect shot of us sitting there with our baseball caps on, watching the game.

In front of the photo, preserved in a glass box, was a foul ball that Dad had caught at another game. After the game, he'd gotten it signed by a couple of players, then he had handed it to me. I had given it back to him saying, "You keep it, Daddy."

I remember the big grin on his face at that moment.

"Those are great pictures of you and your dad."

I turned to see Austin standing there.

"I thought you left," I said in surprise.

He held up an envelope. "Your mom reminded me to pick this up from the kitchen counter."

"I hope she's paying you a fair wage."

"Oh, it definitely helps. I had to cut back on my hours at work because of school."

"Oh, yeah. Law school."

"Rose told you, huh?"

"She told you about me having MS. Fair's fair."

He smiled. "Yeah, I finally took the leap this year and decided to go."

"Congratulations."

"Thanks," he said.

His smile was giving me goose bumps. Or maybe I had them because he moved closer to me.

Looking down at the photos with me, he asked, "So are you a baseball fan?"

"No, I just liked going to the games with my dad when I was a kid."

He said, "It looks like you had fun," and in my head I went back in time.

I did have fun. I think I was five when Dad took me to my first game. I didn't understand the rules, not even for the next few years, but I loved hearing the crack of the bat and the cheer of the crowd.

It was exciting just being at the stadium. And the food there was the best! Dad and I would each have a delicious ball park hot dog, the way we both liked them, with ketchup and mustard, and we'd share some yummy French fries or popcorn. And I got to have pop, which Mom wouldn't let me have at home until I was twelve. Dad's only rule was that it had to be orange pop or root beer.

Dad would get his favorite game snack - the roasted peanuts - and I'd get a warm soft pretzel. I would scrape off some of the salt and pull the doughy pretzel apart in pieces that slowly stretched off, and I would eat each piece individually, taking bites whenever the crowd cheered.

Through my thoughts I heard Austin say, "You look cute with your little baseball cap on too."

I think I blushed. "Thanks. I think Dad had me wearing one before I started teething."

With a laugh he said, "Yeah, dads are like that. Mine signed me up for pee wee football when I was two. Mom divorced him a few years after that."

"Oh, I'm sorry."

"It's cool. We're all still on speaking terms."

We smiled at each other, and then he said, "Okay, now I'm really going. See you, Tess."

"Bye," I said, watching him leave.

I couldn't help checking out his great butt.

Mom called the next week to demand I come over to help with her scrapbooks. I drove over a while later, trying to convince myself it would be fun.

In the back yard I saw Austin in the flowerbed, his knees deep in the dirt. His skin was getting a bit tanned.

I walked over to him. "Now she's got you planting flowers?"

He squinted up at me through the sun.

"Yeah, I volunteered for the job."

I snickered, kneeling down next to the flowers.
"Nasturtiums. Yuck."
He laughed. "You don't like them?"
"She gets them every year. They're so boring."
"What flowers do you like?" he asked.
I let my cane fall, picked up a little shovel, and started to absentmindedly dig in the dirt.
"I love roses," I said gesturing to Mom's rose bushes at the other end of the L-shaped flower bed. She has her namesake flower in white, pink, and red.
"And lilacs. I wish we had some here. And I like those orange lilies. The tall ones. They're about to come up in the front yard. They seem to be all over the neighborhood."
"Yeah, my grandparents have those in front of their house too," he said.
"Which house is theirs?" I asked.
"It's the kind of grayish wood, contemporary style on the other side of the street."
"Oh, I love that house!" I said. "It's interesting."
"Yeah, they bought it because it's different."
"Are they your dad's parents?"
"My mom's."
Mom came out of the house then. "Hi, Tess. Are you planting too?"
"Yeah," I said.
"Well, I have all the pictures lined up for the scrapbooks when you're ready."
Austin smiled as I stood up to give Mom a hug. I glanced at the bird feeder.
"Did you get the bird seed?" I asked her.

"No, I forgot."
Austin looked up. "I'll bring some tomorrow, I promise."
I plopped back down to help him plant.
"Don't stay out here in the heat too long," Mom cautioned.
"I won't," I said.
After she walked away Austin asked, "Are you sure you don't want to go in? It's cooler."
"Yeah, but there are scrapbooks in there." I made a grossed out face.
He laughed. "I guess you prefer the nasturtiums."
"Yeah, I mean, I do like gardening," I admitted.
I took a plant out of its little container and put it in the hole I'd dug. It felt good to be outside getting my hands dirty, despite the boring flowers.
"Do you want some gloves?" Austin offered, gesturing to Mom's gardening bucket.
"No, that's okay," I replied.
He seemed impressed. "I never met a woman who was okay with getting her hands dirty."
"I don't mind. I just love the outdoors," I said with a shrug. "I always have. I was a tomboy as a kid."
"Yeah, I could see that in that picture where you're hanging off the maple," he said with a smile.
I giggled. "I fell off my bike the day before that and my mom had to patch me up. So she was freaking out taking that picture, yelling at Dad not to let me fall."
He chuckled, then he commented, "She still looks out for you."

"Yeah, always the nurse," I said. "I'm the daughter and a patient."

He nodded. "My mom's like that. She's a teacher, so she always helped me with my homework when I was a kid, and she still offers to help me with it now."

"What does she teach?" I asked.

"Fifth grade."

"Were you in her class?"

"No. She teaches at a private school for girls. But if I had a sister, *she* probably would've been. I'm lucky Mom didn't put me in a dress and a wig so I could go there," he laughed.

I giggled again. "Do you have any brothers?"

"No," he said. "Just me."

We planted in silence for a minute, then two squirrels ran by, and we watched them chase each other around the yard until they disappeared into the trees behind the garage.

After that I brushed a non-gloved hand over my perspiring forehead, and looking at me, Austin grinned.

"What?" I asked.

He pointed and said, "You've got dirt on your forehead."

"I guess that means it's time to go in," I said with a laugh, and I pulled myself and my cane up off the ground.

"Fine, just leave me out here," he wailed in jest, and I laughed as I walked to the house.

Inside I got cleaned up in the half-bath by the laundry room then joined Mom in the kitchen for cookies and lemonade.

Austin came in when he was done planting and in typical guy fashion, he washed up at the kitchen sink. I poured a glass of lemonade for him as he approached the table.

He smiled and said, "Thank you."

He took a couple gulps while Mom got him some cash from her purse.

He thanked her, and she said, "No, thank *you* for planting them for me. I appreciate it."

"No problem," he said. "I guess I'll stop by after work tomorrow with the bird seed."

He turned to me and said, "Thanks for helping me with the flowers, Tess."

He gave me a little wink, and I smiled at him as we all said goodbye. After he left, Mom said, "He's so sweet, isn't he?"

"Yeah," I said.

Very sweet, I thought.

I had physical therapy the next morning. Those PT people wore me out, so I sat at home the rest of the day, hanging out with Pokey and eating junk food.

I went to Mom's the day after that. She wasn't home, and the bird feeder was still empty.

"Poor birdies," I said. "Mom isn't feeding you. I know you eat bugs and stuff, but you deserve your seeds too."

I let myself into the house. In the pantry I found a big bag of bird seed. Austin had come through.

I carried it outside to the maple and tore it open. I clumsily poured some into the feeder and then poured a little on the ground. Then the whole bag fell from my hands, and I stooped to pick it up.

Birds were already gathering at the feeder. They flew past me, a few even landing not far from my feet to dine off the ground.

I started to think of Dad as I watched them, and then the tears came. I watched the birds and cried. A cardinal showed up and looked at me as if to ask if it was okay for him to join the feast.

"Help yourself," I told him through my tears. He began to peck at the ground, stopping to look up at me again a few times.

It was oddly comforting.

Before I fell asleep that night I thought about sitting on the ground planting flowers with Austin two days earlier, and then I thought of that little wink he'd given me before he left.

My brain wandered into a fantasy then where the two of us were lying in the grass and all sorts of flowers were falling down on us. We jumped up, I tossed my cane aside, and we started running around the back yard, chasing each other like the squirrels, hiding behind the trees and shrubs, and then finally landing back in the grass in front of the koi pond, where we started kissing, and a few fish popped out of the pond to watch us, like we were in a movie.

In the middle of the night, I woke up from my recurring dream, and I bolted up in bed with the sudden realization that I'd been focusing on the wrong person in my interpretation of it.

It wasn't about the guy; it was about me. Or rather a circumstance of mine. The dream guy whose face I couldn't fully see broke into pieces after my leg started shaking. The MS made him disappear.

After Mark and all his panicking, I had begun to think it might be hard to keep a guy around with MS in the picture. Clearly the recurring dream meant I was still thinking about that.

Things had changed. I wasn't working anymore, I was getting ready to start a new medication, and I'd begun using the cane because of my balance. Mom had even bought me a walker recently – the deluxe model with wheels and a seat. It was still in the box in a closet in my apartment.

I guess reality was closing in on me. MS was more present in my life now, and it was not going anywhere.

I knew now what I really wanted, what I really needed, was one night, maybe two or three, of just sex. One last chance to feel like I was still desirable before I fall apart physically.

No pressure on the guy to stick around, no worries about a relationship ending. And I had someone who I thought would fit the bill.

So that was the objective of a plan I called Operation: Get Austin. As in get Austin to sleep with me.

It was the perfect plan. Or so I thought.

~4~

I had no idea where to start at first. Then it seemed the logical first step was to talk to the woman who'd introduced us.

"Mom?"

She pretends she didn't hear me when I say something that makes her uncomfortable.

I'd called to ask her to ask Austin if he'd – well, you know.

"I'm here," Mom said. "Just had to let the cat in."

This was a new one. And like my Pokey, her fat, female Russian Blue cat Misty never goes outside.

"Mom, come on," I said. "Don't ignore this. It's important."

"Alright," she sighed. "What do you want me to do?"

"I need you to set up a meeting between me and Austin."

"A meeting."

"Yeah. At my apartment."

"Why don't you just meet him for coffee or something?"

"Because this isn't about a date. It's about what I said before."

"You want to sleep with him."

"Sleep? Sure, I guess we'd sleep, after we have sex."
She hates when I use the word sex.
"I don't understand," Mom said. "Why are we talking about you sleeping with him already?"
"Mom, I told you, I don't want to date anyone. I just want to feel desirable, before it's too late." I was on the verge of tears. "I'm using a cane; a walker probably isn't far off. No man will want a woman pushing forty who uses a walker."
"You don't know that, honey," she said. "This is just you letting the MS make you think the worst. You're still very young; you have plenty of time to find someone. Maybe you should talk to a counselor."
I'd done the whole counseling thing after I broke up with Mark.
"Mom, please, I've done the whole counseling thing," I said. "I really need this if I'm going to not 'think the worst' as you put it."
"Well, I'm not comfortable setting Austin up like this," she said. "He does a lot around here, and he's a nice guy. I don't want to do this. I'm sorry."
So I struck out.
I decided to bring in more reinforcements. My sister.

Emily is younger, but she's two inches taller than me. She has the same blonde hair, but hers is naturally curly, which makes me mad. She's married and has two boys – Evan, 3, and Logan, 5. They both have their father's curly chestnut brown hair. The whole family has curly hair. It's annoying.

My nephews are the best though. They came running when I walked in the door that Saturday afternoon.

"Auntie Tess!"

I pulled them in for a hug. Then Em chased them away so we could talk. I told her my idea, and right away she started to interrogate me.

"How do you even know Austin?"

"What do you mean? I've seen him at Mom's. She introduced us. God, Emily, he's not famous."

"I know but, I mean, do you know anything about him? Have you ever talked to him?"

"Yeah, we've talked a little."

"Does he know you have MS?"

"Of course he knows; Mom told him. She tells everybody. Her dry cleaner even knows I have MS."

Emily zoned out then, and I had to bring her back.

"So? Em? Will you talk to him for me?"

She sighed, "I don't know. Don't you know any guys you could go out with?"

"All the guys I know are married. And I don't want to date anyone; I just want the physical thing."

"Why does that mean so much to you? Because of the MS?"

"Yes, exactly."

"Sex isn't that important."

"You say that because you've slept with way more guys than I have. I'm seven years older, and you're like thirty guys ahead of me."

"Shh," Emily warned.

"Why are you shooshing me? Is Steve here?" I looked around thinking my brother-in-law would walk into the room. He's a paramedic for the city, and he works nights during the week."

"No, but the boys..." Emily whispered. "And I have not slept with thirty guys!"

"Whatever," I said.

"Why are you asking me to do this anyway? I barely know the guy."

"You're better at talking to guys. I don't know what to say to him."

"I don't either!" Emily insisted, just as the boys came running in, demanding lunch.

"Can we go to McDonald's and go see Grandma?" Logan asked.

"Sure," Emily said. "Do you want to come with us?" she asked me. "Maybe Austin will be there, and you can ask him out."

I repeated firmly, "I don't want..."

Evan interrupted me with a shout of, "Yay! We're gonna see Uncle Austin!"

I turned back to Emily. "*Uncle* Austin?"

"Yeah, that's what they call him."

"But you barely know him." My sarcasm was heavy.

We piled into my car and went to eat then went to Mom's house.

Austin was there getting ready to cut the grass. Evan and Logan ran over to him as soon as we all got out of the car.

"Uncle Austin!"

Austin called out, "Hey, guys!" and they both giggled as he picked them up, one under each arm.

He looked over at us. "Hey, Emily. Hi, Tess."

We said, "Hi," as Mom came running out of the house and headed straight for the boys.

"You want me to go ask him now?" Emily asked under her breath.

"Very funny," I said.

I looked over at Austin and smiled as I watched him swinging Evan around.

He set him down, and Evan followed Mom and Logan into the house. Still looking at Emily and me, he said, "How's it going?"

"Good," we replied simultaneously.

Emily smacked me on the arm and went into the house.

"What was that about?" Austin laughed.

"Sisters," I said, rolling my eyes. "You're lucky you don't have one."

He shrugged. "I don't know. I think I missed out."

Logan came out of the house then and ran up to Austin. "Uncle Austin, come play our game with us!"

"I have to get the grass cut, buddy," Austin told him.

I motioned with my hand and said, "Oh, just come in for a few minutes. It's hot out here."

He smiled. "Okay."

We went inside, and Logan led Austin into the living room. They sat down on the floor and started playing the boys' little video game.

Emily pulled me aside in the dining room. We spoke quietly.

"Did you ask him?"

"No!" I said. "I want you to do it."

"Why can't you do it?"

"I don't know how."
"I don't either!"
"What do you mean you don't?"
"I've never talked to a guy about it before – it just *happened*!" Emily said.
"You said you'd help me."
"When did I say that?"
We were interrupted by Mom.
"What are you two talking about?"
Again we spoke simultaneously. "Nothing."
Mom sighed and went to the living room.
Emily punched me in the arm.
"Stop that!" I ordered.
"Let's go get the boys some lemonade," she said.
We went to the kitchen and filled up three glasses with ice and lemonade and took them to the living room. I handed Austin a glass.
"Thanks, Tess," he said, smiling at me again.
I followed Emily back into the kitchen. "You have to try to get him alone," she whispered.
"No!" I whispered back. "I'm leaving."
"What? You can't go."
"I'm going home!" I insisted.
She followed me to the back door.
"Tess! Stay! He's into you, I know it. Just talk to him. You can get something going. Maybe you just sneak in a little kiss."
"Not here," I said. "Just talk to him for me, Em, please."
"I don't know what to say!"

"You'll think of something! Just wait until he goes back out to cut the grass and talk to him then."

"No kidding," she said sarcastically.

Mom came into the kitchen and confronted us again. "What are you two whispering about?"

"Nothing," I said. "I'm going home. I'm not feeling so good."

"Okay, honey," Mom said. "I'll call you tomorrow."

"Bye, Mom."

I walked out the door, turning to see Emily scowling at me.

She called me that night.

"So? What happened after I left?" I asked.

"I took him up to my old room and I slept with him," she said.

"Not funny."

"He cut the grass, and then he left."

"Emily!"

"What? My kids were there! Just be patient, Tess. I'll do it another day. I hate you."

"I hate *you*," I said.

"Bitch."

"Slut."

We hung up on each other.

~5~

I thought about what Emily said about trying to get Austin alone. The next morning Mom called me, and I had an idea. A light bulb over my head.

"No, Tess, not the light bulb thing!" Emily said when I called and told her. "That didn't work when you tried it in high school."

"I just want to try again," I said.

She sighed. "Okay. But I don't like this. If you get hurt, I'm sending Steve over."

"Alright. I'm going over to Mom's now."

Mom had asked Austin to come over to retrieve her wedding ring from the bathroom sink drain. She's dropped it in there a few times over the years, and it happened again the night before.

She had told me Austin was coming over at noon.

Okay, so, the "light bulb thing," as Emily called it, was something I did when I wanted this boy I went out with a couple times in high school to...well, you know.

My parents weren't home, and we were watching a show on MTV in the living room. When it was over I asked him to help me change the light bulb in my bedroom closet.

I had the whole thing planned. My bedroom closet is kind of long, but wide enough that you can easily walk into it. It has just one door that slides open, and the floor is carpeted, like the bedroom.

I had placed a straight-backed chair inside, and I asked the boy to hold onto the back of it so I could get up on it and change the bulb. The plan was, after I changed the bulb, I'd ask him to get in front of the chair and help me down, then fall gracefully, but heavily enough to knock him down and land on top of him on the closet floor, thus paving the way for a romantic encounter that would end my status as a virgin.

I even had a stash of condoms in the pocket of one of my sweaters that was hanging on the closet rod.

I remember I had gotten up on the chair and turned so my butt was in front of the boy's face.

I glanced down, and he was looking right at it. I was so excited I could barely get my fingers to work to unscrew the old bulb, toss it into a wastebasket that's in the closet, and put the new one in.

Then, feeling nervous, I had asked the boy to help me get down off the chair. I remember I said, "Stand right in front of it. I'm scared. Please."

He laughed, but he got in front of the chair and put up his hands.

I took hold of them, and with the full force of my body, I lunged forward, intending to push him down and land with a flop on top of him on the floor.

But the boy let go and moved, so I belly-flopped onto the carpet instead.

We didn't go out again after that, and I didn't lose my virginity until college – with some cute guy I met at a party and never actually dated.

So, back to the resurrection of the light bulb thing.

"Call me right after it doesn't work," Emily said before we hung up.

I clicked my tongue and said, "Shut up."

I got to Mom's at noon. The Prius was in front of the garage. Hoping I wasn't too late, I walked into the house. Mom was at the kitchen sink washing dishes.

"Hey, Mom," I said, putting my purse down on the table.

"Hi, Tess."

"Did you get your ring back?"

"No, Austin just went up."

"Oh. Well, I'm going to go get some books from my room. Will you make me one of your famous cheeseburgers? I'm starving."

"Sure, honey. I'll make three – one for each of us."

She did her little pre-cooking smile, and I thought, *That should keep her occupied for a while.*

The closet light bulb was burned out the last time I was in there two months earlier. I hoped it still was, but if not I figured I'd just remove it.

I went up as fast as I could. First I checked the closet light. Yep, still burned out. The wastebasket was still in place. No condoms, but I'm still on the pill, so we were good to go. I moved the chair over, put my cane against the closet door, and went back to the hallway.

I retrieved a light bulb from the linen closet and stepped into the bathroom. Austin was on the floor, his head and shoulders in the sink cabinet.

"Hi," I said.

He slid out from behind the cabinet door. He looked so sexy lying there on the floor in his cargo shorts - one knee up, the other leg stretched out. I noticed a little of his belly was exposed from his t-shirt riding up.

"Hey, Tess!" he grinned.

"Hey. Can you do me a favor and spot me while I change the light bulb in my closet?"

"Yeah. If you want I can change it for you when I'm done here," he offered.

"No, I can change it. I just need someone to stand by the chair. I'd ask Mom, but she's busy making burgers. Do you mind?"

"Okay." He got up and followed me to my room.

"Thanks for doing this," I said on the way. "I'm looking for some old stuff, and it's too dark in the closet."

"Yeah, no problem."

We went into the closet, and he eyed the chair.

"Are you sure you want to get up on the chair?" he asked, then he offered again, "I can get it for you."

"It's okay," I said. "I'll get it."

"You don't like to ask for help, do you?" he observed.

"I don't usually," I admitted.

"Okay, well be careful," he said, watching me get up on the chair as he held onto the back of it. Once I was up, I turned around so my butt was in his face, then glancing down, I saw him looking away.

With a sigh I unscrewed the old light bulb and handed it to him. I told him to throw it in the wastebasket. I put in the new bulb, and the closet lit up.

"Good job," he praised with a grin.
"Thanks," I smiled down at him.
And now for the dismount.
"I hate trying to get down," I shuddered. I really was stuck this time.
"Here, let me help you," he said, reaching up a hand.
"Can you jump down?"
"No," I said shakily. I really couldn't.
He got in front of the chair and held up his arms...
I imagined myself as the fine Victorian lady, her handsome gentleman friend, whom she secretly has an overwhelming, throbbing desire for, helping her down from her horse.
Come on, Tess, you can do this, I thought. *Just put your full body weight into it and knock him down.*
...and then I sort of clumsily fell into them and he eased me to the floor. My flop flopped. Again.
I thanked him as I was berating myself in my head.
"You're welcome," he said. He smiled at me and then walked out of the closet.
Minutes later, Mom had her ring back, and we were all sitting at the kitchen table eating cheeseburgers.
When I got home, I called Emily.
"It didn't work."
"I told you it wouldn't. Did you get hurt?"
"No. He made sure I got down okay. I don't know what happened. It was like I couldn't fall forward."
I told her the whole story.
"You are so bad at this," she said. "You made it too complicated."
"What should I have done?" I challenged.

"You should have jumped him while he was on the bathroom floor."

"That's not me, Emily."

She sighed. "I guess this means you still want me to talk to him for you."

"Yes!" I groaned.

Soon it was July fourth, and Emily insisted I come with her and the boys to see fireworks, since Steve had to work. I hadn't been to Mom's the past several days because my sister was supposedly going to talk to Austin any day now about hooking up with me, which she hadn't yet.

While we were walking out of Emily's house, along with the boys and Steve, I tripped over a toy right outside the side door and fell to the driveway.

Steve rushed over to help me up. "Are you okay? Looks like you scraped your knee. Do you want a band-aid?"

My brother-in-law, the paramedic.

I said I'd take a band-aid, and he went inside then came back out to bandage my knee.

We said goodbye to Steve, got in Emily's car with the offending toy, and headed to a nearby park to watch the fireworks.

As we were sitting in the grass waiting for them to begin, I asked Emily, "When are you going to talk to him about it?"

"Soon," she promised.

"Do you know what you're going to say?"

"Pretty much," she said, which of course meant she had no idea.

I was about to say something else, but then Evan spilled popcorn all over me and the fireworks started.

As I sat there watching them, I thought back to the baseball games. My favorites were always the night games, because of the fireworks.

I used to love seeing the sky above the stadium light up with an explosion of brightness after the game. It was always such a beautiful display, with the most amazing colors. I would close my eyes after a while and just listen to the popping sounds. I could feel them, like they were running through me, giving me chills, goose bumps, and butterflies all at once.

Emily had only gone to one game with us, and then she didn't want to go again because "it was too boring." I tried to convince her to come to a night game because of the fireworks, but she was a brat and didn't want to.

I still went to games with Dad once in a while throughout high school, but eventually that stopped and Dad would just go with his buddies. I went to one last game with him two years ago.

The fireworks that night had seemed more colorful and vibrant than ever before. They had actually brought tears to my eyes. Or maybe I was just emotional about being at the stadium with Dad now as an adult with MS, and feeling nostalgic at the same time.

I remember when I was a kid, Mom once told me she had the sensation of watching fireworks the first time Dad kissed her, and that was how she knew he was "the one."

I waited for that to happen to me with every boy I kissed from the first one when I was twelve, all the way up through the last guy I dated, but it never did.

At some point I decided Mom's romantic fairy tale about the fireworks was just that, a fairy tale, but I love that Dad was her Prince Charming. And I loved hearing about how they met and fell in love.

Now I had my own fairy tale, with no handsome prince, just a wicked witch called MS.

~6~

A week later Emily finally called me to say she had talked to Austin for me. "He's kind of shy about the whole thing," she said, "so he told me he's going to ask you out for lunch when he calls, but he knows you want him to come over to have sex."

I've long been fed up with the cocky type, so the whole shyness thing was welcome news.

He called that Friday, just before noon.

"Hi, Tess. This is Austin. I hope it's okay that I'm calling you. Emily gave me your number."

"Yeah, that's fine," I said. "How's it going?"

"Good. How are you?"

"I'm good."

There was an awkward silence, then he asked, "So, I was wondering if you've had lunch yet. Maybe we could go somewhere?"

Lunch. Wink, wink.

"Yeah, that sounds good," I said. "I haven't had lunch yet."

"Well, how about if I come over and we can decide where to go?"

"Sounds great," I said, and I gave him my address.

He said he'd see me in twenty minutes. I would have jumped for joy if I could still jump.

I went to the bedroom to get ready. Tingling in anticipation, I put on my only once-worn white lace corset with the garter straps and the matching panties.

"Damn it, damn it!" I muttered as I struggled to put on my thigh high sheer white stockings and attach them to the straps.

Lastly, I threw on a lavender short-sleeved button down blouse over the ensemble, planning to slowly remove it as soon as he came through the door.

Austin knocked on the door exactly twenty minutes after we'd hung up.

I slinked to it, and doing my best Mae West pose, I called, "Come in!"

Austin opened the door, smiled, and said, "Hi." Then he took one step inside, and before I had a chance to shed the lavender blouse, he looked down from my face and saw my lack of other clothing.

"Oh!" he cried. His eyes widened, and he quickly turned to look at the wall. "You're not dressed yet!"

"Why would I be?" I asked in my best seductive voice.

"Ah – should I come back, or...?" He started to pace like a caged lion. "I could wait out here I guess."

He threw a confused glance over his shoulder then turned back to the wall.

"You're still in here. Why are you not going to get dressed?"

I was confused. "Austin, I think we've gotten our signals crossed," I said. "Isn't this what you came for?"

"What?" he practically shrieked. "No! I..." he turned around, then back again. "Can you put something else on?"

With a heavy sigh, I trod out of the room to my bedroom. I pulled off the blouse, stockings, and corset and threw on a t-shirt and shorts. All I could think the whole time was, *I'm going to kill my sister.*

I walked back into the living room, where Austin was now sitting on the couch with his head down.

"You can look now," I grumbled.

He looked up as I came to sit. Pokey was on his lap, rubbing against his hand like he was in love with the man.

"Your cat is very friendly," he said as if the whole last three minutes hadn't happened. "Your mom's cat never lets me pet her."

"Yeah, Misty hates everyone," I said. "Not my Pokey, though, he loves everybody, don't you Poke?" I asked, rubbing his head as he purred loudly.

"His name is Pokey?" It seemed like Austin didn't like that name.

"Yeah, short for Slowpoke," I said.

We sat there quietly for a minute before he asked, "So, do you still want to go to lunch?"

Still? "Yeah, sure." My stomach was grumbling now.

"Where would you like to go?"

To this place called Tess's Bedroom. (I didn't say that.)

What I said was, "There's a great sandwich shop around the corner. We can walk there."

"Cool," he said, lifting Pokey and setting him aside. He stood, and my eyes went straight to his cargo shorts and sexy legs again.

We walked to the sandwich shop two doors from the corner of my street in the opposite direction of the coffee shop, making small talk about the weather, the flowers in the containers on the street, and his job at the grocery store.

After we ordered he asked, "So, should we talk about what happened at your apartment?"

"Probably not," I said, still fuming at Emily.

"Okay," he said, and we sat there quietly waiting on our drinks. Then I decided one of us should say something.

"How are your classes going?"

He cleared his throat. "Pretty good. The summer session's over after next week."

"That's great."

"Yeah."

The waitress brought our drinks, and we made some small talk about my nephews and Pokey versus Misty.

"Do you have any pets?" I asked him.

"Not at my apartment, but I have a dog at my mom's."

"What kind of dog?"

"He's a boxer. His name's Beau. Short for Beauregard."

He took out his phone and handed it to me. "That's him," he said with a look of pride.

I gazed at the close-up photo of Beau gaping at the camera, his head tilted to the side.

"Aw, he's so cute!"

"Thanks. He's a real ham," Austin smiled as I gave him his phone back.

Then the waitress, who was around our ages, brought our sandwiches, but she forgot Austin's potato salad and walked away before he could tell her.

He tried to get her attention three times as I nibbled on my fries. Finally, as she walked by he said, "Miss?"

She came back and gave him a sugary grin. "Why are you so obsessed with me?" she kidded.

Austin was a bit befuddled, and I couldn't help but giggle at the way he was looking at her.

"Just kidding," she said. "What do you need, hon?"

He asked for his potato salad.

"Oh, I'm sorry!" the waitress said. "I'll go get that right now for you."

"What's funny?" he asked me after she left.

"Why are you so obsessed with me? That line was from the movie *Mean Girls*," I explained.

"Oh yeah, right. I remember that."

"You've seen it?"

"Yeah. In high school, this girl I dated made me watch the DVD with her."

"Was she a mean girl?"

"Yeah, she mostly was," he recalled.

The waitress came back with his potato salad.

"Here ya go. Sorry about that," she apologized again.

"That's okay. Thanks," he said. Then he asked me, "What about you? Were you a mean girl in high school?"

I threw a fry at him.

"I guess so," he laughed.

"I was...somewhere in between nerd and mean girl," I said. "And I suppose you were the quarterback?"

"No," he smiled. "Far from it."

"What about Pee Wee football?"

"I mostly sat on the bench," he admitted. "High school was photography club and drama club. I played Romeo."

"I'll bet you were great," I flirted.

I was hoping to light a fire that didn't start earlier, but he just kind of blushed and asked, "Did you date the quarterback?"

"No," I laughed. "I think he was a halfback or third back or whatever. And no, I wasn't a cheerleader."

He chuckled. Then he asked, "College?"

I told him about leaving after sophomore year because it was stressing me out.

"Like, really stressed out," I told him. "I was having panic attacks."

"Wow. What was your major?"

"Business. How about you?"

"English."

He told me he'd taught at a literacy organization but got laid off a year ago.

"Did you ever think about going back?" he asked.

I sighed. "I did for a while, but now it's too late."

"Maybe not," he said. "I mean, there are online classes."

"Yeah," I agreed. "But I think maybe the business world just wasn't for me."

He seemed to realize he'd hit a nerve, so we ate in silence for a minute, and then he shifted to another topic.

"So, when's your birthday?"

"December fourteenth. When's yours?"

"December ninth," he answered, wide-eyed. "We're just days apart!"

"My mom told you my birthday, didn't she?" I asked.

"No, she didn't," he swore.

"But she told you how old I am. She told me you're thirty-two."

"Yeah. And you're thirty…?"

How cute, I thought. *He's acting like he forgot.*

"Seven," I said.

"Well, you don't look a day over twenty-seven," he said, smiling.

"Twenty-four, but I'll take it," I teased.

"Okay," he laughed. "And I may be younger, but my body creaks like a guy in his fifties."

I doubted that, and I wished I could get proof.

Thankfully, the waitress brought the check at that moment. Austin dug out his wallet, handed her some cash, and told her to keep the change.

We asked for containers to take the rest of our huge sandwiches home, and after she brought them we packed up.

"This was nice," Austin said.
"Yeah," I agreed. But I was still mad at Emily.

As we were walking back to my apartment he asked me, "So what *was* that all about when I got to your place?"

I hastily threw together an explanation.

"My ex called me and said he might stop by today, and I was just getting ready to make him jealous."

He looked around as we entered the building and he joked, "Do you think he's here now? Should I be worried?"

"No, you can take him," I said, patting his arm.

He grinned. "Your sense of humor is so refreshing."

Not what I wanted to hear as we approached my door.

"Do you maybe want to hang out again?" he asked.

That was better. Maybe I could fix this mess and get Emily to do her part this time.

"Yeah, sure."

"So I'll call you?"

"Okay."

He smiled. "Okay."

I was hoping for a kiss, but he sort of awkwardly put his arms around me and hugged me.

Even more awkwardly, I said, "Do you want to come in and...have...something to drink?" In my head I was cringing: *What is wrong with me?*

"Thanks, but, I have to go to work in a while," he said. "Sorry."

"That's okay."

He gave me another hug as I thought, *Oh, for God's sake!*

"Take care," he said with a smile. "I'll see you soon."

I said, "Okay," and he left.

I practically slammed my apartment door. I threw my purse down on the kitchen counter, took out my phone, and dialed Emily's number. I heard an answer and I immediately went after her.

"Emily! What the hell?"

"Auntie Tess?"

It was Evan's little voice.

"Oh! Hi, Evan, honey," I sang. "Can you put Mommy on the phone?"

I heard Emily in the background.

"It's Auntie Tess. She sounds mad," Evan told her.

Emily came on the phone. "Hey, Tess."

"Emily! What did you say to Austin?" I demanded.

"Okay, I know it's not what we talked about…"

"What. Did. You. Say."

"That you wanted him to ask you out."

I could hear her cringing.

"Emily," I sighed.

"I'm sorry, Tess, I totally choked. I couldn't do it."

"Damn it," I said.

"So what happened?" she asked.

"Well, after I made a fool of myself answering the door in lingerie…"

"Oh, no, Tess, you didn't."

"I did. And he freaked out, and then I got dressed and we went to the sandwich shop."

"So he didn't run out the door after seeing you in your lingerie?" Emily joked. Then getting serious she said, "You guys went on a date – that's not so bad."

"That wasn't the point of this," I reminded her. "I don't want to get involved with anyone so they can run out the door when my MS gets to be too much for them."

"Are you talking about Mark?" she asked. "Didn't you break up with him?"

"Yeah." I plopped down on a stool at the counter, put my head in my hands, and groaned, "God, today was a disaster."

"Don't be so negative," Emily said. "Did you guys kiss?"

"He hugged me."

"Aww! Did he ask you to go out again?"

"No, he said he'd call me."

Suddenly I heard my nephews in the background on the call. It sounded like Evan was crying.

"Uh-oh. I have to go," Emily said.

"Okay. I'll talk to you later."

Damn it, I thought as I hung up. Emily wasn't going to get off that easily.

I needed a latte. I headed down to the coffee shop and found Brad sitting at a table with Sara. I recognized her short brown bob haircut as I walked over.

"Hey, Brad. Hi, Sara," I said.

They both looked up and said "Hi," and right away Sara held up a catalog open to a page of wedding invitations.

"Which one do *you* like, Tess?"

I peered at the page. "They're all gorgeous."

Sara sighed. "I know. I can't choose!"

Brad got up. "The usual, Tess?"

"Yeah," I said following him to the counter.

"Wedding plans – pain in the butt," he laughed as he rang up my order.

I wouldn't know, so I just smiled. I went to sit at my table by the window.

Sometimes I used to wonder if Mark and I would've ended up getting married. Then I'd think we probably would have gotten divorced.

After Brad brought my latte and biscotti, he went back to sit with Sara. The coffee shop was fairly empty, so I could somewhat overhear their conversation.

He said something about writing the invitations on notebook paper, to which she responded, "Ah – no."

I laughed to myself at hearing them laugh. I glanced over and saw him reach across the little table to lay his hand affectionately against her cheek, and I heard him say, "I love you so much."

Then Sara turned her head, kissed his hand, and said as she smiled and gazed at him, "I love you too."

I'll admit I was jealous of them.

That Sunday, I went to Emily's, where Logan and Evan were playing in their little inflatable pool in the back yard. Steve was standing there with the hose, adding water to the pool and occasionally stopping to squirt the boys, causing them to squeal and shriek.

Emily and I grabbed popsicles out of the freezer and went to sit on lawn chairs near the pool.

As we sat there enjoying the sweet, cold treats, she asked if I'd heard from Austin.

"Not yet," I said.

"Are you going to go out with him again?"

"No," I said.

"Why not?"

"Because, once again," I sighed in frustration, "that's not what this was about. You need to help me fix this."

"So you still want me to play pimp?"

"Don't say it like that," I chastised. "Help me."

"I still say go out with him again. It'll be your second date, and that puts you one date closer to the third date – the sex date!"

"I've never done it on the third date," I said. "I make him wait until the fourth."

"Of course you do," Emily sighed.

"Mark didn't want to do it until the eighth date."

"You're kidding."

"I'm serious. I thought maybe he was a virgin."

Emily snickered.

"But when we finally did it, it was great," I said. "The cheater didn't want to do it until the sixth date – that should've been a red flag."

I clicked my tongue in disgust at the memory of him. "I still can't believe I was with him for all those months and he was cheating on me."

I looked at Emily. She wasn't listening. She was gazing over at Steve, who had his eyes fixed on her as she was suggestively sucking her popsicle.

"More water, Daddy!" Logan cried.

Steve pressed the sprayer that was hanging from his hand pointed toward his feet, and he got himself all wet.

"I'm going home," I said with a sigh.

Emily ran after me as I was walking to the car.

"Tess, wait!"

I turned around. "What?"

"I'm sorry," she said. "I'll try again if you want."

"Never mind," I said, "It was a dumb idea."

"I still think he's into you."

I leaned against the car and looked down at the ground.

"Are you into him?" Emily asked.

I opened the car door. "It doesn't matter."

"Tess, come on. Don't be like that!"

She threw up her hands as I started the car and backed out of the driveway.

After I ate lunch my phone rang. It was Austin.

"How's it going?" he asked.

"Good. How are you?"

He told me he was on a break at work, and then he said, "It's supposed to be cooler on Wednesday. They're saying seventy-five. I have the day off, and I wanted to see if you maybe want to go for a bike ride?"

"I can't ride a bike anymore," I told him, thinking he should've assumed that.

"But you don't have to," he said. "It's a bike with a sidecar."

"What?" I asked in surprise.

He explained, "My friend Matt works for the park system at the bike rental place in Grovewood Park. He builds bikes too, and he made one with a sidecar to add to the rentals. He sent me a pic of it. I can send it to you if you want."

"Okay," I said. Then my phone buzzed and I looked at the picture of a bright green bike. It was from a distance, so I couldn't see it very well, but I could see the matching sidecar attached to it.

"I've never seen one of these," I told Austin.

"Do you want to come with me on Wednesday to check it out?" he offered.

I looked at the picture again, and the words, "Okay, sure" just dropped out of my mouth.

Austin said he'd pick me up at noon on Wednesday, and after we hung up, I looked at Poke and asked him, "What's wrong with me?"

He looked at me as if to say, "How should I know?"

~7~

The bike rental place at Grovewood Park is between two bike path signs. We got there around twenty after twelve, parked in front of the little building, and walked past a row of shiny bikes of different colors chained to a bike rack.

Austin's friend Matt very much looked like a bike guy – tall and slender, with a blond man bun and a scruffy beard.

Austin introduced us, and Matt shook my hand and said, "It's great to meet you, Tess. Let me show you guys the bike."

He led us over to the bright green bike, which had a helmet perched on the seat. Looking at the sidecar, I saw it contained a black leather seat that had a seat belt attached. I was more interested in the outside than the inside though.

Matt was telling Austin it was about a twenty-minute ride around the inner loop trail, while I was still examining the sidecar.

"So do these things ever come flying off?" I asked Matt.

"No way," he said. "It's bolted on nice and tight. Perfectly safe."

He pulled on it to demonstrate.

"It's like riding in a car. You can belt yourself in with the seat belt, and just keep your feet on the floor," he cautioned.

"What do you think?" Austin asked me. "Want to give it a try?"

I did. I hadn't ridden a bike in years, and the weather was gorgeous. It was the perfect day for a ride.

I said, "Yeah," and he smiled.

I handed Matt my purse and phone as Austin helped me into the sidecar. I made myself comfortable on the smooth leather seat.

He picked up the seat belt and said, "Here, let me get this for you."

I looked up at Matt as Austin attached the seat belt, and he smiled at me.

"You okay?" Austin asked.

"Yeah, this is great," I said. I ran my hands over the seat while he walked around to the other side of the bike.

I looked at Matt again and saw that he had my purse on his shoulder and the phone camera pointed at me.

He said jokingly, "Okay, Tess, play for the camera, baby."

Austin stepped back and gave Matt a look of reproach, but I leaned back in the seat and held up my arms, giving Matt a big, open smile.

"Perfect!" he said, then he pointed the camera at Austin and said, "Get on the bike, man. Let me get another picture."

Austin put on the helmet and climbed onto the bike, then we both smiled as Matt took the photo.

"Alright, you guys. Have fun," Matt said, handing me back my phone and purse. He walked off and waved to us as Austin started pedaling.

A few seconds after we got on the trail, he looked over and asked, "So, is it comfortable?"

It was much more so than I had expected. "Yeah, very comfortable," I said.

As the bike's tires whooshed quietly over the smooth concrete, I imagined myself as the Victorian lady again, her handsome coachman driving her home, where she would convince him to stay to tea, and they would fall into each other's arms, shed their clothes, and make love unabashedly on the carpet on her parlor floor.

Austin broke into my fantasy to mention the weather.

"It turned out to be a pretty nice day, huh?"

"Yeah," I replied.

I sat back, enjoying the spectacular view of the woods. They're so beautiful and peaceful. The sun was peeking through the trees, and a soft breeze was blowing through my hair.

"This would be great in the fall when the leaves change color," I commented.

"Yeah, we'll have to come back then," Austin said.

His words gave me an uncertain feeling. I thought about it for a moment, but then I brushed it away and continued enjoying the ride.

I asked him to stop so I could grab a few pictures. As we sat there, a doe came out of the woods and got close to the trail, but before I could take a picture of her, she bounded back into the trees.

We rounded the last bend of the loop, and then a few minutes later we pulled back up in front of the bike rental building.

Austin helped me out of the sidecar, and then with his arms around me, he lifted me off the ground and spun in a circle.

Setting me down after this animated hug he said, "That was so great, right? Did you have a good time?"

Oh, but did I wish we were talking about something else. Still, I had thoroughly enjoyed myself.

"Yeah, it was fun," I said with a smile. He got my cane and purse from the sidecar and handed them to me as Matt came over to us.

"How was the ride?" he asked us, to which we replied it was great, and Austin complimented him on the bike.

He and Matt shook hands and said something about maybe seeing each other at some upcoming event, then Matt shook my hand and said, "Nice meeting you Tess."

"It was nice meeting you too," I said.

Austin and I got into the Prius and he asked if I was hungry.

I was. So he drove to the snack bar in the park.

I used the restroom, and then I walked out to find Austin at a picnic table with our burgers and fries in red plastic baskets and our soft drinks.

He jumped up to help me sit at the picnic table and he leaned my cane against it.

As we were eating, I was enjoying the amazing view of the creek downhill from the snack bar.

Then as we were throwing out our trash, I noticed some people walking on a path that appeared to go downhill.

"Does that lead to the creek?" I asked Austin.

"Yeah. There's some stone steps down there that go to it," he told me.

"Can we go see?"

"Yeah, if you want. The hill isn't steep, but I can help you down if you need me to."

I said, "Okay," and we went to the path. Austin held my arm as we went down.

It was just a short way to the steps at the bottom. When we got there I saw that they had pretty thick rises and there was nothing to hold on to. There were only maybe five steps, but I wasn't going to be able to do it.

"I'll hold your hand," Austin said.

I was too uneasy, and worried about the poor shock absorption in my legs. I was thinking I'd slide down on my butt like a toddler, when Austin had a better solution.

"I could carry you on my back," he offered, "if you want to go. But we don't have to."

Perhaps too eagerly, I handed him my cane and said, "Let's go."

"Okay, let's do it," he grinned.

Oh, if only.

He turned around, put his strong arms behind my legs, and lifted me onto his back. I held on happily as he carried me down the steps. At the bottom, he carefully lowered me to the ground and we walked to the creek bank.

I gazed around, taking in the beauty of the trees, the sunlight glistening on the water, the rocks in the creek, and the pebbles under my feet. I listened to the water gurgling along, while Austin picked up a rock and tried to skip it over the creek.

I watched him from a few feet away. The rock just went kerplunk into the water. Austin turned to smile at me.

"I haven't done this since I was a kid."

I smiled. He picked up another rock, held out his arm, and then sent it flying into the creek, where it skipped three times.

He looked back at me again, and I clapped. I took my phone out of my purse and asked him to try another one.

"Oh, you're going to record me?"

"Just this one," I said.

He reached down for a rock. "Okay, now the pressure is on," he kidded. He turned back to the water.

"Ready?" he asked.

I hit record and said, "Go!"

He sent the rock sailing into the creek, and this time there were four skips.

"Yea!" I cried.

Austin grinned at me. "I didn't think it would work."

"You're good at this," I complimented.

"Aw, thanks," he said as he bent down to pick up another rock.

I stopped the recording and snapped a few pictures of the scenery as he tried a couple more. I turned to take a picture of the stone steps, getting a side view of them coming out of the trees.

Turning back, I said to Austin, "Smile!"

He looked at me and smiled as I snapped a picture of him, and then I turned the camera on myself and took a silly selfie.

Looking around he said, "Too bad I left my phone in my car."

"I'll send them to you," I told him. "I mean, I don't do social media."

"Yeah, I hardly ever use it anymore," he said. "So don't worry. I won't post them."

"Well, I mean – you can if you want," I said. "You should post your rock skipping video."

He smiled and came to stand beside me. "Let's take a pic together."

We both smiled up at my phone, and I took the photo. I was confident he wouldn't be posting that we were in a relationship.

After a few minutes we went back to the steps, and as I stood there looking at them from the bottom I told Austin I could climb up.

"Are you sure?" he asked. "I can piggyback you up."

"Yeah, I have an easier time going up steps than going down," I told him. "It's a weird MS thing. But you can hold my hand."

We smiled at each other and joined hands, then I walked up the steps with him, giving my legs a good stretch.

Going up those steps, I felt a little like I used to, when my body performed normally and I still had enough energy. It was flowing through me in those moments. It wouldn't last, but it felt great.

When we got back to my apartment, I was exhausted.

"Thanks for the fun day," I said as I opened the door.

"I'm glad you had fun," Austin replied. He hugged me, then he asked, "What should we do next time? Do you like slam poetry? Or maybe we could go rollerblading?"

He grinned.

I half-heartedly laughed, but my thoughts were racing. *Next time. Oh, God, we're dating. We can't be dating. I don't want that*!

I said, "Um – why don't we just play it by ear? It depends how I'm feeling."

"Okay," he said. "I'll call you, or maybe I'll see you at your mom's and we can maybe hang out after?"

"Yeah," I smiled.

He reached out and gave me another hug. I was getting tired of hugs. He left, and I actually sighed with relief.

Later I looked at the pictures from the day. I smiled at the one Matt took of me in the sidecar, and the one of Austin on the bike, and I wistfully swiped through the pictures I'd taken of the trees along the trail.

I got to the video of Austin skipping the rock, and I watched it over and over.

"I didn't think it would work" and "You're good at this" played on repeat for a while.

I swiped through the pictures I'd taken of the creek, and I caught a glimpse of Austin in one of them, getting ready to skip another rock. I cropped the photo so he took up most of it, and I saved it for myself.

I texted Austin the video and the other pictures, and after a few minutes, he texted back a smiley face with: *Thanks!*

I waited a minute to see if he would text something else, then I tossed my phone aside.

Ten seconds later, the phone buzzed.

A new message read: *Skydiving?*

I laughed and replied: *LOL. Definitely not.*

He texted back another smiley with: *OK. Good night.*

Good night, I texted.

I got ready for bed, turned on my fan, and lay down with Pokey nearby. I leaned my phone up against the bedside lamp, set to the photo I'd saved of Austin.

As I gazed at his bare arms and legs and handsome profile, I let a fantasy take flight. I filled in the rest of his unclothed body and created a setting for our lovemaking with my imagination.

We were standing on the creek bank by a huge brass bed that was covered in white bedding, a light wind blowing through our hair. He put his fingers on my cheeks, we kissed, and as we slid onto the bed, the wind picked up, and the scene changed to a secluded beach in front of the ocean, and the waves were crashing against the rocks as we kissed rabidly, running our hands all over each other, the white sheets flapping in the wind around us.

Lying in my bed, with one of my hands otherwise occupied, I reached over and ran the index finger of the other over the phone screen, up Austin's legs to his butt pressed against the cargo shorts, then up his arm to his shoulder and neck, then over his wavy hair with the breeze blowing through it.

I gasped and shuddered as a surge of pleasure ran through me, and then Pokey got spooked and jumped up onto the nightstand, knocking over the lamp and phone.

"Pokey!" I yelled as he ran out of the bedroom. He runs so rarely, he crashed into the door on the way, and I burst out laughing.

The next day I had lunch with a friend from high school. Meredith. Tall. Thirty-seven. Married. Two kids. Seriously, that's how she talks when she describes people.

We get together a couple of times a year to catch up. I met her in front of the sandwich shop, where she was standing there in typical Meredith style - all glammed out with her Hollywood shades and designer handbag.

She's not snobby though. She hugged me, saying with a girlish squeal, "Tessie! You look so fabulous!"

"So do you, Meredith," I said, recovering from the squeeze.

"Thank you, sweetie," she said. Then noticing my cane, she cried, "You're using a cane now? I like it!"

"Yeah, I don't," I sulked.

"But it's pretty! Think of it as an accessory," she said as she opened the door for me.

Our waiter was a slim, dark-haired guy in his twenties.

I ordered a turkey club; Meredith ordered the corned beef.

The waiter said he'd be right back with our drinks and then walked away.

"Cute," Meredith remarked as she watched him.

I sighed and shook my head. "You never change, Mer."

"Hey, I'm allowed to look. Tom does."

She started in talking about her husband Tom, who she repeatedly says is the "best husband in the world," then the waiter came back with the drinks.

"Thanks, sweetie," Meredith said as he set them down.

He smiled at her. "You're welcome."

She watched him walk away again. Okay, so did I. He was cute. I also spotted the Mean Girls waitress from my lunch with Austin. She gave me a quick hello as she walked by our table.

"Hi," I said.

"Friend of yours?" Meredith asked.

"I've been in here a few times getting takeout," I said.

I didn't want to tell her about Austin. It was bad enough I had to listen to her talk about the best husband in the world.

The waiter brought our food a few minutes later, and Meredith did this smile thing she does, where she acts like you've just given her the most beautiful piece of jewelry.

"Thank you! This looks wonderful!"

"Enjoy," the waiter said.

We dug into our sandwiches, and Meredith told me about all the stuff her kids had been doing lately. After that we dragged out some old memories from high school, and then the conversation took a dark turn.

"So, are you seeing anyone, Tess?"

"No."

"Oh, I know someone who'd be perfect for you! Attorney. Forty-one. Divorced. Handsome."

"No, really, I'm not looking right now."

"Why not? Are you secretly getting married?"

"No. Definitely not."

"Okay, well, if you change your mind…"

"I won't."

"He has a sister. Bi. Pretty. If you're looking for that now."

"No. I'm not."

She looked at me with that concerned friend look.

"Are you alright, Tess?"

"Yeah," I said, trying to sound convincing. "I've just got this infusion in a few days and I'm just a little nervous about the new medication."

"Oh! I know this doctor! You'd love him! Pediatrician. Forty. Great with kids. His divorce is almost final."

I said, "No, Meredith, really…"

Our cute young waiter brought the check.

"How about him?" Meredith asked when he walked away. "No ring!"

"Stop!" I laughed.

"Tess, you're gorgeous, you could have any guy you wanted." She looked over at our waiter talking to another customer. I knew she'd attack him if she weren't married.

"I'm giving him a huge tip," she said.

And thus ended lunch.

~8~

It was infusion day. Emily drove me to my appointment. She was thrilled when I told her about the bike ride with Austin.

"That's great, Tess! One more date in the books."

"It wasn't a date," I argued.

"Did he hug you again?"

"Yeah," I sighed.

"I think it's cute that he's so affectionate with you!" she crooned in delight.

"Yeah, it's adorable."

She reached over to squeeze my hand.

"Em, put your hand back on the wheel," I said.

I didn't want to tell her that Austin carried me down the steps to the creek, lest she'd drive off the road from the excitement.

She dropped me off at the medical building, and I headed up to the IV room, walking past the exam room where I'd seen Dr. Tanner a few weeks earlier. The door was closed, but I could hear him talking to another patient.

In the IV room I made myself as comfortable as possible in one of the big light blue vinyl hospital chairs. I pulled up one of the little side trays and set down my phone and the bottle of water I'd brought with me.

After a nurse stuck a needle into one of my veins, I was ready for an hour of getting chemicals infused into my bloodstream. Then I'd have to sit there for another hour so the nurses could make sure I wouldn't have a negative reaction to the chemicals.

After I'd been sitting for a while, Dr. Tanner appeared in the doorway.

"Hey, Tess," he said.

I smiled up at him. "Hi, Dr. Tanner."

"How's it going so far?"

"So far, so good," I joked. "I hope it stays that way."

"You'll be fine, just keep up that smiling," he said, to which I smiled again. Then giving me his sexy doctor smile he said, "Take care. I'll see you in a couple months."

"Okay. See ya," I said, wistfully watching him go.

Right after he walked away I had a little fantasy where he burst into the room bare-chested, wearing tight black pants and carrying a sword. He used it to slay the evil nurse-witch who was trying to poison me, and then he quickly pulled the tip of the sword through some IV tubing that was binding me to the chair, freeing me, and we ran from the room.

In my mind I was now wearing a white princess dress that billowed as I ran with him down the hallway. We went through a hospital room door into what turned out to be a room in a castle.

As we gazed into each other's eyes, he lifted me into his arms and carried me to a carpet in front of an enormous fireplace. He lowered me to it and then said, "Okay, let's check your blood pressure."

"What?" I said, and I turned to see the nurse standing there holding a blood pressure cuff.

Damn! She came back to life.

I was counting down the minutes left before the nurse could let me leave, when Austin walked into the room.

"Hey! What are you doing here?" I said, stunned to see him.

"I saw Emily at your mom's, and she told me you were here. She asked if I could pick you up. Your mom was out, and she has the boys...anyway, I hope it's okay with you."

"Yeah, it's okay," I assured him.

He took a seat in one of the empty blue chairs. The nurse came over to take out my IV, and he looked away.

"Are you squeamish?" she asked him.

"Yeah – not a fan of blood," he said.

She chuckled and told me I was good to go.

We walked out to the parking lot, and Austin helped me into the Prius.

Before starting the car he said, "I have a gift for you."

He reached behind his seat and then handed me a baseball player bobble head.

"They've been selling these at the store, and they were almost gone. I knew he'd be perfect for you."

I gasped, instantly and completely charmed.

"Aw – this is so cute!" I said. "Thank you."

"You're welcome," he grinned. He started the car and said, "Let's get you home."

I needed a latte. "Can we stop at the coffee place at the corner of my street first?"

"Sure."

He drove there, at one point politely asking how my infusion went.

"It was okay. I didn't lose too much blood," I joked.

He laughed, but then he got serious.

"So how have you been feeling, in terms of the MS?"

"Not bad – just bothered by this heat," I said.

"Yeah, it's been brutal the last couple days."

After a few seconds he said, "It must be rough, generally speaking. How do you handle it?"

I told him I just take it day by day, like I have since the beginning.

"You're so strong, Tess," he complimented me. "Honestly, I really admire your strength."

I looked out the window, feeling a tear in my eye. "Thank you."

Luckily we were approaching the coffee shop.

As we walked in, Brad looked up with surprise at seeing me with a guy. Since the place opened, I'd always come in alone.

Austin grabbed a fruit punch from the cooler.

"I'm not really a coffee person," he explained.

I introduced him to Brad, and they shook hands as I pictured them as medieval knights, fighting in my honor as I, the princess, sat on a throne watching.

"Usual, Tess?" Brad asked as if it were necessary.

"Yeah, but just the latte though," I said. "And to go. I just had my infusion."

I held up my bandaged hand.

Brad nodded. "You doing okay?"

"Yeah, it wasn't bad," I said.

He got my coffee and sent us on our way, after telling me to take it easy.

Austin seemed surprised that Brad knew about the infusion, but he didn't say anything. He drove me around the corner to my apartment building and helped me inside, carrying my latte and the bobble head after he shoved his fruit punch into a pocket of his cargo shorts.

In my apartment, I kicked off my canvas slip-ons then sat on the couch and dropped my purse and cane to the floor. I reached for my latte, and he handed it to me, then he sat on the couch and put the bobble head on the end table.

I took a sip of my latte then leaned back, prompting Pokey to saunter over and jump up onto my lap and start purring. I set my cup on the coffee table and then lay down in a fetal position, pulling him close. I looked over at Austin sitting just inches from my feet.

"Tired?" he asked.

"Yeah," I sighed.

He got up. "Well, I'll get out of your hair. I hope you feel…"

I interrupted softly, "No, please stay for a little longer."

He sat back down with his back against the cushions and after a minute he reached over, his hand brushing against my bare foot. He started rubbing my leg, and I felt a quiver of excitement run through me as his fingers glided over my skin.

I wished his hand would go up further. I wanted to feel his hand go under the leg of my shorts. I wished he'd pull them off. As tired as I was, I wished he'd take me right there on the couch in front of my cat.

He must've sensed it, because he drew his hand away and sat forward.

He sipped his fruit punch, then he looked back at me to ask, "Can I get you anything? Are you cool enough?"

Managing a weak smile I answered, "No, thanks, and yes."

He gave a little chuckle.

I said, "I think I just need to lie down for a while."

He stood again. "Alright. Get some rest. Call me if you need anything, okay?"

"Okay," I murmured, moving onto my back and stretching my legs out over the spot he'd just vacated. I tugged at the hems of my shorts to expose my thighs and looked up at him.

I wanted him to lean down and kiss me. I wanted him to say, "I'm staying" and go for it, but he didn't. He just gave my bare shin a final pat, and with a "Take care," he left.

I dug my phone out of my purse.

"Hey, sis," Emily answered.

"No hug today. Still no kiss. He just rubbed my leg a little."

"That's sweet though."

"Emily, this isn't going to work. I appreciate you sending him to pick me up, but I just think I should give up on this whole thing."

"Why?"

"Because I don't want a buddy, or a nursemaid." I sighed. "I don't know. Maybe I should go to a bar and pick up some random guy. Have a one-night stand with a total stranger."

"No, Tess. That's not you," she said.

"You're right," I admitted with a sigh.

"It seems like you're having fun with him," she offered.

"But I don't want to date - anyone."

"Maybe you could be friends with benefits?"

"That's just it," I said. "There are no benefits. I've dropped hints – and nothing. This was about me wanting to feel *attractive*, to feel like someone wanted to be with me for my body, before it's too late. I've said that from the beginning."

Emily's last bit of advice was: "Then just tell him that."

I knew she was right.

~9~

"Tess!" Brad greeted me enthusiastically as I came into the coffee shop. "Are you going to be at the street fair tomorrow night?"

Our neighborhood's annual street fair is the highlight of the summer. It runs a few blocks, starting at the corner in front of the coffee shop. The whole area is lit up by strings of lights at night. There's food, art, and music, and all the local businesses stay open until midnight.

This was going to be Brad's inaugural street fair, but I'd gone a couple of times with Emily and my nephews.

"Yeah, if it's not too hot outside," I replied. "Are you working?"

"Yeah, I'll be here," he said. "Hopefully I'll be able to get out to the street for a while."

He was super busy with customers, but he brought my latte and biscotti out to my table and touching my shoulder he said, "I hope I see you tomorrow night."

Later, back at the apartment, my phone rang. It was Austin wanting to know if I was planning to go to the street fair. He'd seen the flyer at a nearby bookstore.

"I figure since it's right outside your door, you might be going," he said. "It looks like it'll be a good time."

"Yeah, I went a couple years ago with Emily. It was great. I'm not sure if I can go to this one though because of the heat."

"How about if I come by and we go just for a while after dark?"

"Yeah, maybe."

"And we don't have to stay long. I have to work the next morning anyway. I mean, if you don't feel up to it, I understand."

I agreed to meet him in front of my building at ten o'clock the next night.

I put on my lightest clothes that night – a sleeveless white blouse and my shortest shorts, which are made of gray linen.

I walked out of my building as Austin was about to come in. Even though it was dark, the air was steamy, but I figured I could handle it for a while.

The sounds of the fair and the aroma of all the fair goodies were enticing.

As we walked around the corner, I said I wanted to stop into the coffee shop to say hi to Brad.

I went up to the counter as Austin hung back a little.

"Having fun?" Brad asked.

"We just got here," I said, and Brad and Austin waved hello to each other. I asked Brad if Sara was coming.

I was stunned when he said, "We broke up."

"Oh, no!"

"Yeah, the wedding's off."

"Oh, Brad! I'm sorry to hear that," I said. I felt so awful for him.

He responded solemnly, "Thanks, Tess."

I looked back at Austin, and I saw a few people had lined up behind me, so I told Brad I'd better let him get back to work and I'd see him later.

"Yeah, go have a good time," he said, giving us a smile.

We stepped back out into the muggy night and the crowded street. We stopped to look at some handmade jewelry and some t-shirts, but didn't buy anything.

Then Austin spotted a turquoise painted rock on the next table, and he asked the woman how much it was. He bought it and handed it to me saying, "For you."

I held the smooth, sort of oval-shaped rock that fit in the palm of my hand and ran my thumb over it. The turquoise at the center looked like a mystical pool, and tiny turquoise flowers were painted here and there around it.

I smiled at Austin. "Thank you. It's so pretty."

He smiled back. "You're welcome."

I zipped the rock into a small compartment in my purse for safekeeping, and we moved along.

"We'd better get something to drink," Austin said.

We stopped to get lemonade, which was then followed by fries and elephant ears.

"I won't hold it against you if you want to get a beer," I told Austin as we passed a beer vendor.

"No, they overcharge," he smiled, and we sat down to eat.

Two blocks away there was a stage, and after a few minutes a really great-sounding band started playing.

"Want to go over there and catch some music?" Austin asked, speaking loudly above the crowd noise.

"Sure!" I said. I figured he was probably bored just sitting around eating.

We got up from our small table and headed toward the stage. The music got louder as we approached. At first I bopped around to it a bit, but after a couple of songs the sweltering heat, compounded by all the bodies in close proximity to us, was too much for me.

"I need to leave!" I yelled in Austin's ear. "This heat is getting to me!"

"Okay!" he yelled back, and he took my hand to lead me through the throng in front of the stage.

I let go of his hand after a minute, and as we were approaching the coffee shop, I began to feel weak and dizzy.

The heat had become so thick it was oppressive, and I was soaked with sweat. I felt like I was trudging through the desert, meanwhile all the sounds and the people milling about were closing in on me. Then the area began to move in a circle in front of my eyes. I collapsed to the sidewalk and lay there as the world spun around me.

"Tess!" Austin cried.

I saw Brad come running out of the coffee shop and heard him say, "Oh my God, Tess!"

A few other people gathered around us. Austin asked if he and Brad should take me inside, but I didn't want to move or to be moved because of the vertigo.

Austin called 911, and the next thing I knew an ambulance had arrived and two paramedics were at my side. As I looked at them, I felt less dizzy. They helped me to sit up and asked me what happened. I explained about having MS and how the heat had affected me.

Austin was standing there holding my cane and looking worried. Brad brought me a bottle of water.

I took a gulp, and then the paramedics asked if I wanted to try to stand. I said, "Yes," but as they were lifting me a pain tore through my left ankle, and I cried out.

They lowered me back down and lightly touched my ankle, which was painful.

They lifted me onto a stretcher. They wouldn't let Austin ride in the ambulance, so he gave the paramedics my cane and called out to me that he'd call my mom, go get his car, and come to the hospital.

The ambulance sat for a few minutes while the paramedics took my vitals and asked for all my personal information. Then we were on our way.

At the emergency room, the paramedics spoke to the staff at the nurses' station. Then they transferred me onto a gurney in one of those little curtained off areas, and after wishing me well, they took off, leaving me in the hands of a hot male nurse.

He smiled at me before he shined a flashlight in my eyes and took my blood pressure.

"So you got dizzy, huh?" he asked.

"Yeah."

"Does that happen a lot?"

"No," I said. "I think it was the heat."

He felt around my ankle, and I winced.

"Can I have something for the pain?" I asked.

"Yeah, I can get you something," he said. "Hang tight, I'll be back soon, okay?"

"Okay," I sighed.

I watched him leave. His butt looked great in his scrubs.

Austin rushed in about ten minutes later.

"You scared me," he said. "Are you okay?"

"Yeah, but my ankle hurts. The nurse is going to bring me something for the pain."

"I called your Mom. She was at her friend's house but she's on her way."

I thanked him, and he took a seat by the gurney.

We were quiet for a moment, then he said, "I guess we stayed too long."

"I guess," I murmured.

Just then Brad came in. "Tess. Oh, man, don't ever scare me like that again!"

"Sorry," I said, smiling as he put a hand on my shoulder.

And after that, my brother-in-law, the paramedic, in uniform, came from around the curtain.

"Tess. I thought that was you. What happened?"

I told him everything, then I introduced him to Austin and Brad.

Hot nurse came back in next and kind of looked curiously at these three guys, then coming to my bedside he gave me my pill and said, "I have to start an IV for you."

Austin and Brad both turned away.

Steve said he would call Emily to let her know what happened.

"Thanks," I said. Then I asked the nurse if I was going to need an x-ray.

"The doctor will probably order one," he said.

Mom came in as I was surrounded by all these men.

"Steven!" she said, surprised. "Did you bring her in?"

"No, I was here bringing in someone else," Steve told Mom.

She smiled at Austin, and then she grabbed my hand without the IV.

"How are you feeling now, Tessie?"

"I'm not dizzy now, just tired, and my ankle hurts," I said, looking up at her.

"Did you give her something for the pain?" Mom asked the nurse.

He nodded, and I confirmed that he did.

Mom peered at my ankle. "Well, it doesn't look bad."

"Don't touch it!" I cried.

"I won't," she assured me. "Has the doctor been in yet?"

"No, I'm still waiting."

"Shouldn't be much longer," the nurse said, and he left again.

Mom turned her attention to Brad and said, "Hello. I don't think I know you."

I introduced them. "This is Brad from the coffee shop by my building. Brad, this is my mom."

He shook Mom's hand and said, "It's nice to meet you, ma'am." Then he said to me, "I've got to get going. I have to help close down the shop."

"Okay," I said. "Thanks for coming."

"Sure. Take care of yourself, Tess."

After he left, Steve then said he had to leave too, so it was just me, Mom, and Austin.

Then came the moment I'd been waiting for.

Mom looked at me and groaned, "Why on earth did you go out in this heat?"

"It was just for a few minutes," I said like a five-year-old, prompting Mom to shake her head in frustration.

Austin jumped in to rescue me saying, "I convinced her to go down the street. It's my fault."

The doctor decided to make an appearance then, and he and Mom conferred over my ankle.

I winced in pain again as the doctor felt it.

"I think it's just twisted," he said, "but we'll check for a fracture."

Hot nurse came in a minute later to wheel me to the x-ray room. When I got back to my little curtained area, I sat down on the gurney next to Mom. Austin was slouched in a chair looking very tired, so I told him he should head home.

He dragged himself to his feet and came to the gurney to hug me goodbye.

At first Mom and I sat wordlessly after he left. Then she asked if he and I were dating.

"No," I said firmly, "and we aren't sleeping together."

"Okay," Mom said, realizing I didn't want to talk about it. She called Emily to check on the boys, who were both recovering from stomach flu, then she made me talk to her for a few minutes.

Thankfully, the doctor came back then and said I didn't have a fracture. He sent me home with the advice to just rest and stay off my feet for a few days.

Mom drove me home, where I lay down on the couch and fell asleep. And I had the recurring dream again.

Austin called my phone from outside my door late the next day. The one good thing about my ankle hurting was, at least for a week, he wouldn't ask me out.

I was at the kitchen counter feeding Pokey.

"Yeah, come on in," I told him, and I tossed my phone aside.

He walked in, and when he saw me he rushed over to lower Pokey's bowl to the floor. Poke meowed in objection and jumped down from the counter.

Austin grabbed my cane that was leaning on a stool.

"Here, let me help you to the couch," he said. "You need to rest."

"I'm fine," I insisted.

He took my arm anyway.

"Can I get you anything?" he asked after I was settled on the couch.

"No, thank you," I replied.

He looked around. "Do you need another pillow to prop up your foot?"

"You don't have to fuss over me," I told him.

He sat down. "I know. I just feel like it's my fault you got hurt. It was too hot for you to be out."

"It's not your fault," I said. "I wanted to go."

He smiled. "Can you just let me have a little guilt and tell me how much pain you're in?"

"It's excruciating," I joked. "Worst pain ever."

"Thanks," he chuckled.

"Actually," I said, "there is something you can get for me. I'd really like a latte."

He got up from the couch. "I'll be right back."

He left and came back a short time later. He handed me my latte and said, "Brad says 'Hi' and he hopes you'll be better real soon."

"Aww. That's nice," I smiled.

He sat again as I sipped my latte, and then I decided to put him to work a little.

"Can you get me that other pillow now?" I asked. "I think I do need it."

"Yeah, sure," he said, jumping up off the couch.

He went into my bedroom to get the pillow, and I thought it was sad that this was his introduction to the room. He brought the pillow to the couch and gently lifted my leg and slid it underneath.

I felt my whole body tingling as he carefully lowered my leg to the pillow.

"How's that?" he asked.

"Much better, thanks," I said.

"What else? Do you need me to paint your toenails?" he grinned.

I laughed. "No, thank you. But you could brush Pokey for me. He loves it."

"O-kay," he said, with an odd look. "Where's his brush?"

"In the drawer under the kitchen counter."

Austin fetched the brush and called to Pokey, who came running. He jumped up onto the couch as Austin sat down again.

He started to brush him a little tentatively, but Poke was loving every second of it, so he brushed him harder.

Watching Pokey rolling around on Austin's lap and purring loudly, I couldn't help but feel jealous.

After a couple of minutes, I stretched out my arms and yawned.

"I better let you get some rest," Austin said. He set Pokey aside. "Call me if you need anything else, okay?"

"Yeah," I said, giving him a little smile as Poke came to cuddle with me.

I was waiting for a kiss from Austin, but once again I was disappointed. He rubbed my shoulder and told me to get some rest, and then he left.

I scratched Pokey under the chin and said, "Your love life is better than mine, Poke."

A few days later I was pain free, so I went over to Mom's to feed the birds. As I stood watching them fly around the feeder and gather for drinks at the pond, my phone rang. It was Austin.

"How are you feeling?" he asked.

"Much better," I said.

"That's good. I'm on my way to my grandparents' house. It's their anniversary, and they're having a cookout – nothing big, just family. Do you want to come with me?"

I didn't really, but I said, "Oh – um, I guess so. I'm actually at my mom's house right now."

"Awesome! I just got off work. I'll swing by and pick you up in a few minutes, okay?"

"Sounds good," I said, trying to seem excited.

I hung up. "Shit," I muttered. Now I had to meet his grandparents on yet another date.

~10~

Austin picked me up and he drove down to the gray contemporary eight houses from Mom's on the other side of the street. We got out of the car and walked past the door to the built-in garage then into the back yard and up a few steps to a huge, gorgeous cedar deck.

Austin introduced me to his grandparents, Robert and Lillian, two of the nicest people I've ever met. They got me a can of pop from a cooler, and we all sat down at a glass-topped patio table.

We made the requisite small talk, which included Robert asking about my cane.

"You have one too, I see," he commented, indicating his own cane.

"I have MS," I explained.

"Oh, we're sorry to hear that," Robert apologized.

I appreciated Austin not telling them.

Lillian asked, "How long have you had it?"

"Seven years," I replied.

"I'm sorry," she said. "My younger daughter, Austin's aunt, has it too. She says it's a real pain in the ass."

We all laughed, and I looked over at Austin, who looked down at the table.

Then Robert said, "What do you say we get this grill fired up, Austin?"

They got up from the table and went to the gas grill. Austin got it started, and then he went inside and came back out with a platter of meats.

After a few minutes of being on the deck, I needed a break from the heat, so I asked Lillian if I could go inside.

"Austin?" she called. "Will you take Tess inside so she can cool off?"

Austin opened the sliding glass door and brought me into the big, sunny but blissfully cool kitchen.

"Better?" he asked.

"Yeah, this is much better," I said.

I asked him to show me around, so he led me through the downstairs area.

The whole place had laminate flooring, white walls, and high ceilings with recessed lighting. The tall angled windows let in loads of sunlight.

In the foyer, I gazed up at a fantastic rectangular glass chandelier and an open staircase with a cool-looking metal banister.

I got lost in my imagination again for a moment, envisioning Austin carrying me up those steps the way he'd carried me down the stone steps to the creek, and then laying me down on a bed surrounded by white curtains blowing in a breeze in an all-white bedroom.

"This house is amazing," I said, leaving the fantasy.

"Yeah, I used to love sliding around on these floors in my socks as a kid," he laughed.

So now I was stuck with that image in my head.

On the way back to the kitchen, he let me peek into the downstairs master bedroom, which had its own door leading to the deck.

"There's a bathroom down the hall," he told me as I sat at the kitchen table and leaned my cane against a chair. "I'll be right out here on the deck if you need anything. I just have to help them cook."

He looked at me apologetically.

"That's okay, go. I'll be fine," I assured him.

He touched my shoulder before going back out.

I glanced around the kitchen. When my eyes went back to the sliding glass door to the deck, I saw Austin standing at the grill with his grandfather. He turned around and smiled at me. I smiled back then looked down.

As I was surveying the kitchen and playing around on my phone, I heard voices outside. It sounded like new guests had arrived. After a couple of minutes, the sliding door opened and a woman came in from the deck.

As I turned in my chair she asked, "Are you hiding in here?"

"No, it's just so…hot out."

The pause was because I saw that the woman, who appeared to be in her fifties, was pushing a walker.

"Oh, I know," she laughed. "It's been so horrible." She eyed my cane. "I'm Austin's aunt, Linda. You're Tess."

"Yeah," I said. "How'd you know?"

"Austin told me he brought a friend named Tess. So you have MS too?" she asked me.

"Yeah," I said, wondering who out on the deck had told her.

She grabbed two bottles of lemonade from the fridge and handed me one. I thanked her as she sat at the table.

"How long have you had it?" she asked.

"Seven years. You?"

"I'm going on twenty now. God, I wish I still was," she laughed.

I smiled. Then I noticed the wedding ring on her finger. I asked her how long she'd been married.

"Almost sixteen years," she replied.

"Do you have any kids?" I'm nosey.

"We have a fourteen-year-old son. He's hanging out with his friends today. Teenagers. I guess it's not cool to celebrate your grandparents' anniversary."

"Yeah," I commented.

We sat there not talking for a moment.

"Gosh, that food smells so good," she said.

"It does," I agreed, inhaling the delicious smell wafting from the deck.

Lillian and Robert came in at that moment to get some food from the fridge. He was leaning on his cane, and she shuffled beside him.

As they took out the covered dishes, Linda asked, "Do you need any help, Mom, Dad?"

"Oh, no, we're fine," Lillian sang. "Don't trouble yourself."

"It's no trouble, Mom," Linda sighed, getting up. She took a dish from Lillian, who had one in each hand, and placed it on the seat of her walker, then they went back out together through the sliding door Austin had opened for them.

Linda came back in and sat down, shaking her head.

"Mom acts like I'm helpless sometimes," she said. Then smiling she added, "But she knows I'm a tough cookie."

I smiled back.

"And my husband's out there playing chef at that grill," she laughed, glancing back at the door.

I looked out to see a tall, bearded man talking to Austin by the grill.

"Did you know your husband before you got diagnosed?" I asked, being nosey again.

"No. We met about two years after, the year before we got married," Linda said.

I could feel my brain teeming with jealousy. She leaned forward and jokingly growled, "Now, it's my turn to ask questions!"

"Okay, shoot," I said.

"Married? Kids?"

"No. No. I have two nephews though."

"Symptoms?"

"Ah – first it was numbness Like all down my legs."

She nodded.

I continued, "Now I get light-headed and lose my balance once in a while, and I have muscle spasm and fatigue."

"Foot drop?"

"Oh, yeah, that too."

"We could be twins!"

We laughed, and then she asked, "How long have you known Austin?"

"Just since May. He's been helping my mom out."

"Oh – your mother lives down the street, right?"

"Yeah."

"My sister mentioned her to me," she explained. "My big sister who isn't here yet." She glanced out to the deck again and shook her head in mock frustration.

We took sips of our lemonade, then as she set hers down she said, "I think Austin likes you. I mean, more than as a friend."

Like MS, she'd hit a nerve.

"I don't think so," I said, looking down.

"Is that good or bad?"

I shrugged. She could see that I was upset.

"I'm sorry. We can talk about something else."

"No," I said, 'it's okay."

Suddenly I felt like I wanted to talk about everything. It was like we were kindred spirits.

"I mean, that's been kind of a problem since I got diagnosed," I told her. "I had this boyfriend who freaked out about it, and now I guess I feel like guys..."

Linda nodded like she knew where I was going, and then the tall, bearded man came in from the deck with a plate of food and set it on the table in front of her.

"This is my husband, Jim," she said. "Honey, this is Tess."

He shook my hand and gave me a big smile. "Hi, Tess. Can I get you a plate?"

"I think Austin is getting me one," I said.

"Okay. Well, I'm going back out. Some of us are okay in the sun," he teased Linda.

"Very funny," she said as he leaned down to kiss her. "Now get out of here so we can talk."

We watched him go back out, then she said, "I know what you mean. After I got diagnosed, before I met Jim, I broke up with someone. I was really depressed for a while after that. Especially after the MS started to affect my walking. I thought it made me less attractive. But Jim was persistent. And he proved to me time and again that it didn't."

I had never met someone who could relate to what I'd been feeling this whole time. Of course at that moment I was too envious of her to appreciate that.

I didn't want to talk about it anymore. I glanced down at my phone then looked up at Linda. "I have to leave," I said abruptly. "I have to babysit my nephews."

She held out her hand. "Let me see your phone so I can give you my number, in case you ever want to talk."

Reluctantly, I handed it to her. After she typed in her number she asked if she could have mine and used my phone to call hers. As she gave it back, Austin came in through the sliding glass door and over to the table with a plate of food for me.

I got up. "I have to go," I told him. "I forgot I promised Emily I'd watch the boys for a little while."

Surprised, he set the plate down on the kitchen island and said, "Oh, okay. I'll take you back to your mom's."

"It was nice meeting you," I said to Linda.

She reached for my hand and gave it a squeeze. "It was nice to meet you too, Tess," she said. "Take care of yourself in this heat."

"You too," I replied as Austin and I headed to the door.

We walked out to the deck, and I said goodbye to Robert and Lillian, who were disappointed that I couldn't stay for dinner.

"Austin, get her plate so she can take it home," Lillian said.

He went back in and got it, and Lillian quickly threw aluminum foil over it before she and Robert hugged me goodbye.

"It was so very nice meeting you," Lillian said.

"Nice to meet you, Tess," Robert echoed.

"It was nice to meet you too," I said. "And thank you for inviting me. You have a lovely home."

After the goodbyes, Austin and I walked back to the Prius. I was glad to be getting away from all the family gathering overload.

"Why didn't you tell me your aunt has MS?" I asked once we were settled in the car.

"I guess I didn't think of it," he said. "I don't really think of her as someone who has MS."

It was a great answer.

Austin backed the car out of the driveway. "It's too bad you didn't get to meet my mom," he said. "The two of you would've hit it off."

Now he wanted me to meet his mother?

I didn't say anything, so he said, "I feel bad you didn't get to eat. I owe you a meal."

"That's okay, I have one," I said, holding up the plate.

"Yeah, but I mean a real meal, not take-out." He thought for a moment. "How about we go to dinner tomorrow night? Do you like Italian?"

"Yeah."

"Why don't we go to Geraci's? Have you been there?"

I love Geraci's.

"Yeah. That sounds great." I said that with all the enthusiasm of someone finding out they were chosen for jury duty.

"Great," he echoed. "So I'll pick you up at seven?"

"Okay."

We were in Mom's driveway. He got out and opened the car door for me.

"I'll see you tomorrow at seven then," he said as he walked with me to my car. He reached to open the door, but I got to it first.

"Okay. Bye," I said as he gave me another damn hug. He smiled at me and I gave him a little smile before he went back to his car. Relieved that the whole thing was over, I got into mine.

I drove home and ate my take-out meal, which was delicious.

After that I sat down on the couch and looked at the bobble head. Pokey jumped up to sit by me. I scratched his ears and said, "How am I going to say what I need to say, Poke?"

He gave me a meow and settled onto my lap, purring.

"Yeah, I don't know either," I mumbled as I stroked his soft fur.

I needed to figure it out.

~11~

At seven the next evening, Austin knocked on my door. I wasn't ready to go anywhere, but he didn't seem to notice as he came in. Pokey ran up to him, and he stooped down to pet him.

I paced about nervously, my heart thumping.

He stood up. "Ready to go?"

I stopped pacing. "No," I said. "No. I can't."

He looked at me, concerned. "What's the matter?" he asked. "Are you not feeling well?"

The words flew out of my mouth.

"I don't want to go out to dinner. Actually, I don't think we should see each other anymore. Outside of running into each other at my mom's house."

He was taken aback. "Why?"

Now I didn't know what to say. I stood there looking at him. I knew I had to say something, I had to tell him the truth, but before I could, he jumped in, asking a question that completely caught me off guard.

"Is this about you wanting us to have sex?"

"What?" My heart rate jumped, and I was almost literally floored, losing my balance a little as I took a step back.

He caught my arm and then gestured to the couch, where we both sat down. What he said next made my heart fall into my stomach.

"Your mom told me you were feeling undesirable because of the MS, and you wanted her to ask me if I'd…hook up with you."

I looked down at the floor. "When did she tell you?"

"Ah – it was a few weeks ago. I can't remember exactly what day."

"Was it before we went to lunch?"

"Yeah." It was his turn to look down as I turned my eyes back to him.

"Was it after Emily talked to you?"

"No."

I was shaking, and my voice was shaky as I spoke. I'd deal with my mother later.

"You didn't tell me. You knew, and you said nothing."

"I'm sorry, Tess," he said, looking up at me.

"You asked me out because you felt sorry for me."

I could see he was hurt by that statement. "That's not fair," he said. "You know I don't see you that way."

"But you didn't want to sleep with me," I continued. "You don't want to."

"I wanted to get to know you."

"That's a nice way of saying you don't."

"No, I mean I do," he stumbled. "I do, of course. I've *been* wanting to. I just wanted to spend some time with you before getting into all that. And after I talked to Emily…"

"Don't bring Emily into this," I said. "We've spent time together, and you've hugged me, and touched my leg, and carried me at the park..." I was practically shouting, so I calmed down. "But you wouldn't even kiss me."

"I'm sorry," he said again. "Maybe I wasn't sure if you really wanted to get to know *me*. Did you? Was it just about sex?"

I looked away. "I knew this wouldn't work," I muttered under my breath.

He didn't hear me.

"It's okay if you don't want to answer," he said. "I don't want to lose whatever this is between us. We'll stay here, and if you want, we can take that step. We could order in."

He smiled and put his hand on mine, but everything had changed. What I thought I wanted, I didn't want anymore. Not like this.

"Never mind," I said. "You should just go. I'm sorry if I made you feel, I don't know, used or whatever. We just shouldn't do this anymore."

He looked at me, his mouth pressed in a downward turn, his eyes straining to find some glimmer of hope in my face. He took his hand off mine.

"Okay," he said. "If that's what you want."

I said, "It is."

He got up and shuffled to the door. Before he opened it he turned back to me and said, "You didn't make me feel used. I would've asked you out anyway."

After he walked out, I leaned back on the couch and started to cry. Pokey jumped up onto the end table, knocking the bobble head over in the process. I saw it fall to the floor before Poke came to sit by me.

Looking up at me with his concerned expression, he put his paw on my stomach and let out a little meow.

With a sob I pulled him into my arms and pressed my tear-covered face against his fur.

~12~

I went to Mom's the next day. I already knew Austin wouldn't show up there because he had to work. Emily was there though, and we ended up arguing.

First I told them about what had happened with Austin and what he said.

"What happened to, 'I don't want to do this. I'm not comfortable with it?'" I demanded of Mom.

"I'm sorry," she said. "I was just trying to help."

I looked from her to Emily. "You guys talk about me all the time. Why didn't you tell me?"

"I didn't say anything to Emily," Mom said in her defense.

"Well, it doesn't matter," I said. "I'm done with Austin."

I walked to the living room, and Emily followed me, asking, "Why do you do this all the time, Tess?"

"Do what?"

"You push men away."

"I do not push men away!" I yelled.

"You do!" she yelled back. "I've seen you, Tess! You pushed Mark away after you got diagnosed..."

"He couldn't handle it!" I interrupted.

"And there was the guy right after Mark, and the one a couple years ago. And you *know* it's not about the MS," she admonished. "You pushed guys away *before* you got diagnosed!"

I couldn't believe she was doing this. "I'm allowed to stop dating a guy, or to break up with a guy who I can't deal with anymore, or who cheated on me!"

"Okay, I get the cheating, but what does that mean, you couldn't deal with them?" she demanded.

"What difference does it make?"

"See? You can't even come up with a good reason!"

"I don't have to explain myself!" I shouted. "And Austin lied to me!"

"He didn't lie! He just didn't tell you what Mom said."

"It's the same thing!"

Mom walked into the room at that moment and said, "I'm sorry, Tess. I should've told you I talked to him."

"It's not your fault," I said to her. "I just have the worst luck with guys, that's all."

We all stood there for a moment, not saying anything, and then I sank down onto the couch.

Emily came to sit beside me. "You have got to stop comparing every man you meet to Dad."

Tears sprang to my eyes. "I don't do that."

Emily gave me that look she gives the boys when they say they didn't do something that they clearly did.

"Well, I seem to recall after you broke up with Mark, you said to me, 'Why can't I find a guy who's like Dad?'"

I honestly don't remember saying it, but I must have.

I started to sob then.

"I miss him so much!"

Mom sat on the other side of me, and with tears in her eyes she pulled me into her arms.

"We all do, honey. No one was as great as your dad."

No one. I wailed on.

"You don't know what it's like, to feel like you're losing control of your own body. To watch other people your age running around, doing all the things you can't do anymore. I hate it, I hate it so much! I hate that everyone knows there's something wrong when they see me now. I hate that it comes up in every conversation. You can't understand. Nobody understands. Nobody ever understood except Dad!" I blubbered.

"I know, honey, I know," Mom comforted me.

I confessed between sobs, "No guy has ever told me he loved me. Never, not once. Except for Dad."

"Maybe you just haven't been with anyone long enough," Emily suggested.

Mom chided, "Not helping, Emily."

I turned to my sister. "You and Steve were ending your calls with 'I love you' after two months."

"It was 'Love ya' – not the same thing," she argued.

She was amused by that, but I burst into tears again.

"All I wanted was to feel normal again with a guy, and I can't even have that."

"Oh, Tess," Mom said, gripping my hand. "I hate to see you like this. Let me talk to Austin and try to work this out for you."

"No!" I cried. "I don't want to see him anymore. If he's here when I come over, I'll just leave! The operation was a bust, and I'm too upset about it."

"What operation?" Mom asked.

I got up and headed out of the room. Seeing Misty, I followed her into the kitchen.

"C'mere, Misty!" I called, and she stopped. I slowly stooped down, and she actually let me pet her, looking at me as if to say, "I know. Men are dogs."

Meanwhile, I heard Mom and Emily talking.

"What operation? What did she mean?"

"Mom, I don't know."

I left Mom's and I drove to the cemetery to visit Dad's grave. I needed to talk to him, even if he couldn't answer back.

I brought him some peanuts. I sat on the ground and poured out the bag in front of the headstone. I knew the squirrels were going to eat them after I left, but Dad wouldn't mind. He'd love that.

I took a peanut for myself and cracked it open.

"Hi, Dad," I said. "I really need to talk to you. Everything is just so screwed up. I guess I screwed it up. I keep having this dream and – anyway that's not important – I just…"

I started to cry. "I really wish you were still here. Because I know you'd tell me the right thing to do."

I went back in time then, to a day in the back yard with Dad when I told him I broke up with Mark.

"Oh – I'm sorry, honey," he'd comforted.

"I have such horrible luck with guys," I remembered saying. "And now it's only going to get worse. I'll have to tell them; they'll get scared away…"

"You don't give us guys enough credit, Tessie," Dad had said. "We're not all like Mark. Or those other guys you dated…what were their names again?"

"We don't need to speak their names," I had grumbled.

Dad had chuckled at that, and then in a more serious tone he had said, "Don't sabotage yourself, okay? I want you to be happy, Tess. If you get a bad peanut, just throw it away and keep reaching into the bag. Keep looking, keep trying, until you find the right one that will make you happy, because he's out there. And when you find him, don't think about the MS. Don't worry about it. Just be happy."

I came out of the memory sitting there at Dad's grave with a handful of peanuts.

I smiled at the headstone, "Thanks, Dad."

A few days later my phone rang early in the morning. It was Linda.

"I'm taking you to lunch today. I'll pick you up at one. What's your address?"

"Ah, today?" I tried to think of an excuse really fast.

"Do you have plans?" she asked, sounding suspicious.

"No," I admitted. (*Damn!* I thought.)

She picked me up at one in front of my building and drove around the corner to the sandwich shop at my suggestion.

The Mean Girls waitress came over to take our order.

"You've been in here a lot lately," she commented, smiling.

"Yeah, the sandwiches are great," I said.

After we ordered, Linda and I compared notes on our dealings with MS until our lunch arrived. Then as I bit into my turkey sandwich, I froze for a second when Linda said, "So, Jim and I went to Grovewood Park yesterday to look at a bike with a sidecar that Austin's friend Matt made. He told us you and Austin went for a ride."

I wiped at my mouth, swallowed my bite, and set down my sandwich. "Yeah, we did," I said. "Did you guys go for a ride?"

"Just a short one. Jim hasn't ridden in years. He was worn out after ten minutes," she laughed.

I giggled and started to eat one of my fries.

"Matt seemed to think that Austin was 'working hard to impress' you, as he put it," Linda added.

She was smiling and had a twinkle in her eyes, but then she noticed my facial expression had changed.

"Uh-oh," she said. "Did I say something wrong?"

"No," I assured her. I hesitated before saying, "It's just, I told Austin I don't want to see him anymore."

Her face registered surprise then concern. "Oh, I'm sorry to hear that. May I ask why?" she asked.

I couldn't tell her that. I stammered, "It - it's not important."

She studied my face for a moment. "It is. It's important to you, but you don't want to tell me. I understand," she said.

Then with a clap of her hands she suggested, "Let's talk about something else."

We did, and we actually had a nice lunch after that. I thought about how after all these years with MS I'd finally made friends with someone who has it too, because I now felt like we were friends.

"I'm really glad I met you," I told Linda before we got up to leave. "I wish we'd met sooner."

She smiled and raised her glass of pop. "Hey – better late than never."

"Better late than never," I agreed, and we clinked glasses.

~13~

I'd been meaning to check out the new open-air market and grocery in the neighborhood, near the coffee shop, so I walked over on a cloudy afternoon a couple of days after my lunch with Linda.

I bought a reusable canvas bag and a few peaches, strawberries, fresh lemonade, bread, cheese, and turkey. Then I added a separate paper bag with dry cat food and treats for Pokey.

As I was heading to the checkout line, I heard a familiar voice say, "Tess?"

I looked up, and there was Mark, ten feet in front of me. My heart dropped at seeing him – not because of his appearance – he's still handsome, even though his hair is getting gray now that he's in his forties.

I just never thought I'd see him again, this man I blamed in part for my relationship insecurity.

He glanced at my cane as he approached me.

"I thought that was you," he said. "How are you?"

Ignoring his question, I asked in as friendly a manner as possible, "What are you doing on this side of town?"

If he lives around here now, I'm going to have to move, I thought.

He smiled. I remembered how much I used to love that smile.

"You know me, I'm a sucker for a fresh produce market," he said.

He is.

"I was having lunch nearby with a friend. I drove by this place and wanted to check it out. So how are you doing?" he asked again.

"I'm fine," I said curtly.

"You look good."

"Thanks," I replied. "So do you." I was being polite, but he does.

He shook his head in amazement and said, "It doesn't feel like it's been seven years since I last saw you. Has it really been that long?"

I began to wonder if this was one of those fate moments where you run into someone from your past, and you get a second chance.

"Yeah, it doesn't feel like it," I agreed, not sure if I wanted one though.

A good-looking guy around the same age as him approached Mark then and said, "The cheese section looks good. Let's go get some bread."

"Okay. Be right there," Mark told him. The guy started to walk away, and smiling again Mark said to me, "It was nice to see you, Tess. Take care."

"Yeah, you too," I replied, feeling amused.

He hurried to catch up with the other guy. Eighth date. It made sense now. I guess it was good for him that I broke us up. I hope he and his friend are happy.

Walking back home, I saw Brad as he was coming out of the coffee shop. He looked over as I approached.

"Hey, Tess!" he said. "Need a hand with all that?"

"Um, sure. Are you off for the day?" I asked.

"Yeah, they let me leave early."

He took my bags. "Thanks," I said. "I'm just around the corner here. The first building."

"You're closer than I thought," he commented as we walked. "Have you lived around here long?"

"A few years."

To my dismay, he then asked, "So how's your guy? Austin is it?"

"Yeah, but he's not my guy. We're not together."

"Oh. I'm sorry. I just thought…"

"That's okay."

We had reached my building. I opened the door. Brad had hardly broken a sweat carrying my bags. He insisted on bringing them in for me too.

He helped me unpack everything, and I poured us both a glass of lemonade and shooed him over to the couch.

"So what happened with Sara?" I demanded after we sat down and took sips.

He said glumly, "She told me she cheated on me. I guess it happened a couple months ago. He's some guy she used to date. She said they needed closure, and that she's sorry. I told her it's over, and she walked out."

"Oh, Brad, I'm so sorry," I said.

I'd never been this close to him, physically or emotionally. My eyes moved over his face, from his new splash of a beard to his deep brown eyes. He looked like he was about to cry, so I set my glass on the coffee table and put my arms around him. He set his glass next to mine and his arms went around me in return.

The hug went on for a minute. I was beginning to wonder what was going on, then suddenly he was face to face with me again, and his lips met mine.

It was just a brief kiss. Surprised by it, we looked into each other's eyes for a couple of seconds, and then we kissed again, more fervently. After a moment his arms loosened from around me.

He pulled off my t-shirt and his hands caressed my breasts in between kisses – first over the bra, then sliding up underneath it. His touch felt so good.

I lay back on the couch, then he took off his t-shirt, revealing his Adonis chest, rippling muscles, and toned abs. He leaned down and planted his lips on mine again, and then he shifted his half-clothed body in between my legs as we kept kissing. I raised my knees.

He stopped kissing me for a moment and looking into my eyes he said, "You're so beautiful, Tess."

I smiled, and our lips came together again.

My hands were all over his back, getting close to dipping into his jeans to feel his great butt, and then suddenly he had my bra off. I felt exhilarated as our chests pressed together.

A few sloppy kisses later, he moved downward, his lips covering my breasts as his fingers traced my shoulders. I quivered. Then he ran his fingers along my sides, inching down, and I moaned softly as he placed a

trail of kisses down my middle, getting closer and closer...
　I was holding my breath. This was the moment. This was the unbridled passion I wanted, the validation I needed.
　His fingers came to the button of my shorts, and at that moment I realized I just couldn't let him. As much as I wanted to, as much as my body was crying out for him, even though he wanted my body as much as I wanted his, I knew it would be wrong.
　"Brad, stop. We shouldn't."
　He propped himself up. "What?"
　I moved out from under him, swung my legs off the couch, and put my bra back on.
　"What is it?" he asked, putting his hand on my shoulder.
　I brushed aside my hair, and looking at him I said, "We can't do this. I don't want to be your revenge for Sara cheating on you. You should try to work it out with her."
　He sat up slowly and then he said, "I don't know if I can."
　I thought about that day in the coffee shop when I'd seen them at the table together.
　"Do you still love her?"
　He turned to look at me with tears in his eyes again.
　"I don't know. I mean, she really hurt me."
　I put my hand on top of his. "I know. But I've seen the way she looks at you, the way you are together. You were so in love. If you still feel any of that, you have to fight for her. You can't just let her go."

He had turned his head and was looking straight forward, but it seemed like he was thinking about her. He turned his gaze back to me, and he kissed my hand.

"We should've met first."

I smiled again. "But we didn't. I think fate got it right with us though, and I'm really glad we're friends."

"What if fate's wrong about me and Sara?"

I was thinking at that moment about how I'm totally unqualified to give anyone relationship advice, but I plowed ahead purely based on female intuition.

"There's only one way to find out," I advised. "And I'm guessing that when she walked out, she probably wanted you to follow her."

"Maybe," he sighed. He looked over at the kitchen counter, where Pokey was sitting there judging him.

"I guess I'd better go," he said.

He hugged me again, and I had one more moment to feel his skin against mine. We put our t-shirts back on, and I walked him to the door.

"Thanks, Tess," he said.

"You're welcome," I replied. "Thanks for helping with my groceries."

"No problem," he said. "Take care."

He kissed my cheek.

As he walked out I said, "You too."

Inside I was wondering if he would take my advice, and maybe a little part of me was wondering if we should have met sooner.

~14~

Mom called me on Monday the following week. She'd just watched the weather forecast that morning.

"It's going to be ninety degrees all week, so I don't want you going out," she said. "I'm sending Austin over tomorrow with groceries for you."

"What? No, Mom," I objected. "Emily can bring me stuff."

"She has her hands full with the boys. Austin gets off work at five, so he'll probably get to your place around six. I'll give him a list of what to bring you when he comes to cut the grass today."

Gritting my teeth, I said, "Mom, I told you I don't want to see…"

"Misty!" she yelled in my ear. "That cat just ran off with a whole piece of fried chicken. I have to go."

"No! Not the cat excuse again! Mom!"

She hung up. The woman hung up on me.

I sat there, mad at the weather, mad at everything, and wondering if he'd been standing right there while she was talking to me.

Austin knocked on my door a few minutes after six the next day.

I opened the door to see him standing there holding the handles of four paper grocery bags that were filled to the top and a couple of smaller plastic ones.

With a half smile he said, "Hi, Tess."

"Hi," I said flatly.

He brought the bags in and took them to the kitchen. We didn't speak as he unpacked my groceries, and I started putting things into the fridge and freezer. Pokey came running into the kitchen and rubbed against his leg.

"Hey, Pokey," he said, and he reached down and petted him. I quickly popped open a can of cat food and dumped it in Pokey's bowl to take Pokey's attention away from him.

It was spiteful I guess, but I couldn't help myself.

Not to be outdone, Austin went to the closet in the hall with the folded grocery bags and he came back out with the walker box.

"What are you doing with that?" I demanded.

"I'm going to put it together for you," he said as he carried the box into the living room.

"I don't need you to do that," I snapped as I followed him.

Ignoring me, he sat on the couch and opened the box.

"Did my mom tell you to do this too?" I asked in a smarmy tone as he took out the parts.

I stood with my arms crossed as he began assembling the walker, then in a huff I went and plopped down on a stool at the kitchen counter.

I sat there in frustrated silence, just wanting him to leave.

He finished the walker in just a few minutes, and then he rolled it over to me saying, "I know you don't need it, but at least it's ready in case you do."

"Thanks," I said, not at all gratefully.

He sighed. Poke followed him as he went to the kitchen sink and washed his hands. Then he picked Poke up and gave him a hug before bringing him to me and depositing him in my lap.

He walked to the door after that, stopping to say before he left: "You know, Tess, it doesn't matter if you use a cane, or if you'll have to use a walker one day, or even a wheelchair. Because you'll always be who you are, and you'll always be beautiful."

It was the second time in less than a week that a man had said I was beautiful. I hugged Pokey as Austin walked out of the apartment.

I had the recurring dream again that night, only this time things were a little different.

I was in bed with the mystery man again. It was still light outside and my leg still had the tremor, but the guy didn't burst into pieces. He stayed whole, and then I shoved him out of the bed!

As he went over the side, I heard a long "AHHHHH!" like he was falling far down, so I crawled to the other side of the bed and looked over the edge. I grabbed onto it, seeing the guy, face down, plummeting from what looked like the roof of a skyscraper. I was so high up I couldn't even see the street below, just the thin white clouds that surrounded him.

There was a sound like someone had turned off the lights on a soundstage, and it became pitch dark. I was still crouched on my bed, confused and shaken. Then footsteps came out of the darkness in front of me.

A little spotlight came on, and I saw Dad standing there. He was wearing his ball cap and holding the foul ball he caught. He tossed it in the air a little and caught it.

Looking directly at me he said, "Don't sabotage yourself, Tessie. Just be happy."

He turned and walked away after that, tossing and catching the ball as he did.

"Dad, wait, come back!" I called. "Dad!"

All the lights came back up then, and I was at the edge of the bed looking down into the clouds, screaming, "Come back!"

I woke with a start to find myself lying on my stomach close to the edge of the bed and Pokey sitting on the floor, looking up at me with his big green eyes.

"Hey, Poke," I cooed. I moved over and patted the bed. "Come on up."

He jumped up and I ran my hand over him and said, "Did I knock you off the bed? I'm so sorry."

He curled up next to me, purring in forgiveness.

By Saturday, the weather had cooled to below eighty-five degrees, so I walked around the corner for a latte.

Brad was at the counter as usual, but he was locking lips with a woman with short brunette hair. She turned around as they heard me approaching, and I was surprised to see Sara.

"Hi, Tess!" she said.

I smiled and said, "Hi, Sara." Then I glanced at Brad as Sara bounced up to plant another kiss on him.

"I'll see you later, babe," she said, giving his hand a squeeze.

"See ya," he exhaled.

Sara and I said a quick goodbye and "nice to see you," then she and Brad waved to each other as she left.

He turned to me. "Hey, Tess."

I could tell he wasn't sure if he'd see me again.

"So you're back together. That's great," I congratulated.

"Yeah, thanks. It is," he said, easing into a smile. "Can I get you the usual?"

"No, actually, I think I need an iced mocha. Big time."

He was surprised.

I reached into my purse to get some cash, and I felt something in the small zippered compartment. I unzipped it and found the turquoise rock from the street fair inside. I'd forgotten about it.

I held it in my hand, feeling its smoothness and gazing down at the turquoise lake in the center and the little flowers around it.

I paid for my iced mocha and biscotti, and Brad said he'd bring them right out.

"Thanks, Brad," I said.

I went to sit by the window. I took the turquoise rock that was still in my hand and set it on the table.

When Brad came over he set my order down and then he sat across from me.

"I'm glad you're here," he said. "I wanted to thank you for the other day. You were right to tell me to work things out with Sara. I don't know who was more surprised – her that I forgave her, or me that it was so easy to forgive her."

I smiled. "That's awesome, Brad. I'm glad you took my advice."

"Me too," he said. "So I guess things aren't weird between us then?"

"No, we're good," I assured him. "And I'm happy for you guys!"

He grinned. "Thanks. We'll have to start over with the wedding plans, but that's okay. We've got a second chance, so we're gonna take it slow."

I sipped my coffee.

"It's good, right?" he asked.

"It's delicious," I said.

Brad got up and patted my shoulder before jogging back to the counter where a customer was waiting. I glanced at the rock.

As I took a bite of my biscotti, I thought about what he'd said about second chances, and how I'd missed mine.

~15~

There was a knock on my door the next morning. For a second I felt a swelling in my chest. I went and opened the door, and I was surprised to see Emily standing there.

We hadn't spoken since the big argument we'd had at Mom's house.

"Can I come in?" she asked, looking genuinely contrite.

"Sure," I said, and I stepped aside.

She followed me to the kitchen counter, stopping to crouch down and pet Pokey, who was munching loudly at his bowl.

At the counter, I was making breakfast. I finished spreading some cream cheese on a blueberry bagel.

"Can I have one of those?" Emily asked.

"Yeah," I said. I took another bagel out of the bag and set it on a paper towel. I put some cream cheese on it and slid it over to her.

We stood there eating silently for a moment, and then she said, "I'm sorry, Tess. I didn't mean all that stuff I said."

"It's alright. You're entitled to your opinion."

"But it's not my opinion of you," she said. "You're my big sister, and I love you. I've been jealous of you my whole life because you're so perfect, but I love you."

"I'm not perfect," I disagreed. "Not at all. You shouldn't be jealous."

"There's no way I can't be," Emily said. "Since you got diagnosed, I've watched how strong you've been, with everything you've had to deal with. I know I could never be as strong as you, Tess."

"That's not true," I told her.

"It made Dad love you more too," she said with tears in her eyes. "But he always loved you more anyway. And you're not the only one who misses him."

I went to her and hugged her, both of us crying now.

"He loved us both the same, Em. He said it all the time, don't you remember?"

"Yeah. But I still think he really loved you more, and that's okay, because I do too."

We hugged each other tighter.

I held onto her for a long time before I finally let her go. My beautiful baby sister. For a moment I thought about when she actually was a baby and I held her for the first time when she came home from the hospital. I remembered breathing her in, and being so happy that she was finally born and I wouldn't be alone anymore.

I tugged at one of her long blonde curls and kissed her on the cheek, and we went back to eating our bagels.

Emily took a huge bite out of hers, and she got a little cream cheese on her nose. I laughed.

"What?" she asked as I took a paper towel and wiped her nose. Then she laughed too.

We stood there eating as Pokey sat by the sink bathing. We were quiet for a minute before Emily said something about the elephant in the room.

"Are you really never going to speak to him again?"

"Probably not," I said looking down at the floor.

"I was at Mom's on Friday with the boys," she told me. "He was there with his dog. The boys got a real kick out of him."

"That's nice," I said.

She pulled a piece off her bagel, then after a few seconds she said, "He misses you."

"Did he say that?"

She had that sad, serious look.

"He didn't have to."

~16~

It was a Friday, the beginning of Labor Day weekend. It was a cooler day – seventy-three degrees. The long, hot summer was coming to a close.

I ate breakfast then took a shower. I spent my after-shower rest period sitting on my bed looking at pictures on my phone. I laughed at Evan and Logan being goofy and scrolled through pictures of the fireworks on July fourth. Then I got to the ones from the bike ride at the park.

There was the bike and sidecar, the trees along the trail, the creek, the cropped picture of Austin, the stone steps. I swiped forward to the picture of Austin looking at the camera. I sat there gazing at it for a minute before swiping on to my silly selfie and the picture we took together.

Pokey jumped up to sit by me and he looked at my phone. He set his paw right on the screen.

I reached over to pet him. "I know, Poke. I miss him too."

I walked to the park a short distance down the street from my building. It was fairly empty. There were just a few kids running around on the playground.

I sat on a park bench and took long, deep breaths of the cool air. Looking around, I saw an older couple walking down a path across the way from where I sat. He had a cane; she had a walker. His free arm was around her shoulders. I could hear their voices a little and even some laughter as they slowly traversed the path.

My eyes followed them as they headed toward the other entrance to the park.

Seeing this older couple I thought about Mom and Dad, and how they wouldn't be growing old together.

In the back of my mind I heard Mom saying to me, *"You're still very young. You have plenty of time to find someone."*

Maybe I do, I thought, *but what about this monster I carry around with me?*

I saw the old couple stop, appearing to discuss whether to sit on a park bench. They continued on, and then I realized that at some point any couple would both lose some of their abilities as they aged. Robert and Lillian, Linda and Jim, even me and some mystery man in a possible future.

Time and nature would even things out.

~17~

I went to Mom's house on Saturday. It was still cooler out. Emily was over with the boys, and they were making homemade potato chips.

While Mom was heating up the oil, I snagged a few raw potato slices and nibbled them to a chorus of "Ew" from Logan and Evan. After the stove was on for a while it got too hot for me in the kitchen, so I ducked outside.

I went to sit in the grass not far from the maple and laid my cane beside me. There was a group of birds gathered at the feeder and some others below it, dining off the ground. After a moment, the cardinal swooped down to join them.

As I watched him grab some seed, I heard footsteps on the driveway and then Austin's voice.

I felt that swelling in my chest again when he spoke.

"They say a cardinal can be a sign that the spirit of a lost loved one is watching over you," he said.

I looked back at him. "I've heard that."

He came to sit next to me in the grass. We sat there for a minute not talking, even though there was so much that needed to be said.

Finally, he broke the silence.

"I was watching you with the birds on another day too," he confessed, gazing at the maple.

"What day?" I asked.

"The day after I brought the bird seed because your mom forgot to buy it," he replied. "You were filling the feeder, and you poured some seed on the ground, then you dropped the bag. You picked it up and walked away, then you turned around, and the birds came flying over to feast. The cardinal was there then too. And I saw you crying."

I felt a small jolt at those last words.

"So you were spying on me?"

"A little," he admitted. "I had just walked over from my grandparents' house. I saw your mom's car wasn't here but yours was. And then I saw you, but I didn't want to intrude, so I left."

I didn't know what to say for a moment. Then words just came tumbling out of my mouth.

"You could've stayed," I said.

He took my hand in his. A part of me wanted to pull away, but there was something that told me, that even compelled me, to hold on to his hand.

He continued his confession.

"I wanted to. I wasn't sure how you'd feel if you saw me though."

He had his fingers intertwined with mine. My eyes stayed on them as I listened to him.

"I thought about how you looked in those moments over and over after that day. The birds were flying around you, and even though you were crying, it was beautiful. I wished I could've taken a photo of you in that moment."

"But you didn't have your phone?" I teased.

"I didn't have my phone," he said with a smile. "But the image stayed with me, like a photo in my brain. I kept looking at it; I kept wanting to see you. I kept thinking how I wanted to do something just to make you smile."

I had tears in my eyes. He was looking right at them.

Then he said, "And after a while I realized it was on that day that I fell in love with you."

And that's when I started to cry. Austin put his arm around me, and I leaned on his shoulder and slipped my arm around him. I felt like such a jerk for not appreciating his hugs. This was all the physical I needed.

We sat like that, watching the birds, and I wiped my tears with my sleeve.

The cardinal came toward us after a minute or so, pecking at the ground as he made his way with his little talons. Then he stretched his glorious red-feathered wings, his dark-bead eyes focused on us, and his bright red beak opened slightly.

I know it sounds crazy, but it seemed like he wanted to say something to us. Then he turned and flew away.

"Bye!" Austin called out.

I echoed, "Bye!" and waved to our winged friend.

"We'll see him again," Austin said.

"Yeah," I agreed.

He gave me a side squeeze. "I have to go back to work for a couple hours."

I was disappointed he couldn't stay.

Then he turned to me and asked, "Can I come over tonight?"

My heart rate jumped. "Yes, you can come over," I answered with the biggest smile.

He leaned forward and finally, he kissed me. And I saw the fireworks. And heard them, and felt them.

It was truly the best kiss I'd ever had - warm and full - and it felt like his lips were slow dancing with mine. Then our lips pulled apart, almost reluctantly, taking their time. Dare I say it was like pulling apart the soft pretzels at the baseball games?

After that, he stood and held out his hand to help me up. As I got up he reached down and picked up my cane.

He handed it to me. "So I'll see you around eight? And I'll bring some Geraci's."

I smiled and nodded.

Then with a grin he asked, "Will you wear what you had on the first time I came over?"

Laughing, I said, "Yes." And then I fell - into his arms.

We stood there in this long embrace. I felt so good with his arms wrapped around me, holding me tightly. It got to a point where it felt like it was the most natural thing in the world, and just where I was supposed to be.

Eventually he had to let go though. He had to go back to the store. We walked to my car and his body pressed mine against the driver's door. I put my arms on his shoulders as he gave me another fantastic kiss.

After our lips pulled apart again he said, "I love you, Tess."

Those damn tears came back as I said, "I love you too."

He wiped them away with his hand, and then he circled a salty, damp finger around my lips before kissing me once more. Warm tingles danced all over my body as he looked into my eyes, ran his fingers through my hair, and said, "See you tonight."

"Okay," I murmured before he turned and walked off down the driveway, looking back to smile at me.

At the same time Emily came out of the house. I heard Austin say "Hi" to her.

She came up to me and said teasingly, "Looks like someone's getting lucky tonight."

I sighed happily, "Yeah, I can't believe it. And the best part is, he told me he loves me."

Emily gasped and put her hand on my shoulder. "Tess! Oh my God!" She threw her arms around me. "I'm so happy for you! Oh my God!"

"Calm down, Em," I laughed.

She let go and stepped back, clasping her hands together in excitement. "He's so great, Tess. See? I knew you'd get him."

"You did not," I teased.

Her laugh turned into a sigh, and after a few seconds she said, "Steve wants a divorce."

I was floored, in the figurative sense. "What? Oh, Em, I'm sorry!" I cried. I gave her a quick hug before I shifted into protective big sister mode.

"What's his problem?"

"He says he's not sure how he feels about us anymore."

"Asshole! What does that even mean?"

"I don't know," Emily sighed.

"I've never really liked him," I huffed. "Does Mom know?"

"Yeah, I told her. And Steve and I are going to try and work things out," Emily said, showing me my anger wasn't necessary.

"Oh," I said sheepishly. "Yeah, definitely you should try. He is a good father to my nephews. And I know you love him."

"Yeah," she said. "I do."

"So you're okay?"

"Yeah, I'm fine. Either way it'll be fine," she said. "Don't worry about me. Just be happy, Tess."

We smiled at each other.

"I will," I promised. "I already am."

She hugged me again before jogging back to the house.

"I'm telling Mom!" she shouted back to me before she went inside.

I shook my head and laughed a little.

Before I began making my way back to the house I glanced over, and I saw the cardinal sitting between the maple and the garage, looking at me.

"I am. Really," I said to him. Then he tilted his head and fluttered his wings before flying off again.

Epilogue

This isn't a dream. I'm still awake.

The bedside lamp is off now and we're lying in bed in the dark. My lingerie and his clothes are on the floor. My short-sleeved lavender blouse is still in the kitchen, where he took it off me before carrying me into the bedroom.

Austin's arms are holding me close as we spoon, listening to the rain pattering against the window.

He moves a little, and I feel his hand slide down my back, his touch giving me a fresh wave of tingles.

"Tess?" he murmurs, his hand going down further.

I respond with a soft sigh. "Yes?"

Austin leans in, his damp hair brushing against my neck.

I smile as he presses his lips to my ear and whispers, "You have a great butt."

ABOUT THE AUTHOR

Lenore Nicastro wrote her first stories as a child. They were never published – her mom just typed them up and put them into a folder with a picture on it of a seagull in flight against a blue sky. The folder disappeared years ago, but Lenore still holds out hope it will turn up.
She wrote other stories over the years and finally started publishing in 2019. She mainly writes short stories of mixed genres.
Lenore has had MS for over twenty years. She has a Bachelor's degree in Communications and has worked in radio and public relations.
You can find her on Facebook and Instagram under the username, "Storied Existence."

(And if anyone finds the seagull folder with the typewritten pages inside, please let her know.) ☺

ALSO BY LENORE NICASTRO:

Novel –
        The Bellwood Legacy

Short stories -
        Shadow Stories

        Happenstance and other stories

        Storied Existence

Ebooks –
        Skeletons of Bellwood

        Everything Went Dark
        Two Chilling Tales

Printed by Amazon Italia Logistica S.r.l.
Torrazza Piemonte (TO), Italy

54009139R00084